THE STONE CHILD

BOOK THREE OF **THE MISEWA SAGA**

THE STONE CHILD

DAVID A. ROBERTSON

PUFFIN

an imprint of Tundra Book Group, a division of
Penguin Random House of Canada Limited

First published 2022

1 2 3 4 5 6 7 8 9 10

The author would like to acknowledge the
Canada Council for the Arts for their support.

Manufactured in Canada

Library and Archives Canada Cataloguing in Publication

Title: The stone child / David A. Robertson.
Names: Robertson, David, 1977- author.
Series: Robertson, David, 1977- Misewa saga ; bk. 3.
Description: Series statement: The Misewa saga ; book three
Identifiers: Canadiana (print) 2022016570X |
Canadiana (ebook) 20220165726 | ISBN 9780735266162 (hardcover) |
ISBN 9780735266179 (EPUB)
Subjects: LCGFT: Novels.
Classification: LCC PS8585.O32115 S76 2022 | DDC jC813/.6—dc23

Library of Congress Control Number: 2022932473

www.penguinrandomhouse.ca

Penguin
Random House
PUFFIN CANADA

This book is dedicated to Colleen Nelson,
because a bet is a bet.

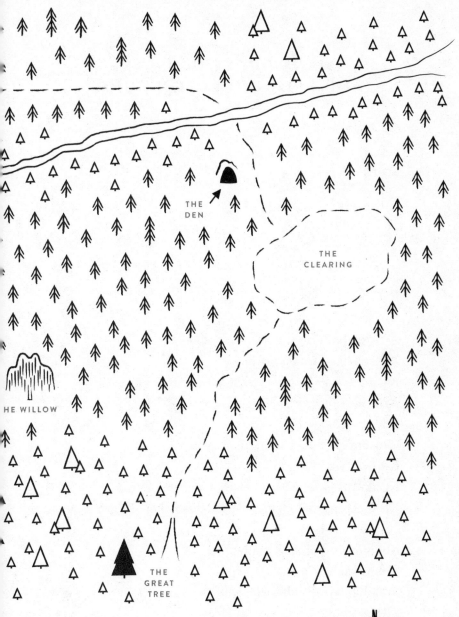

THE DEN

THE CLEARING

HE WILLOW

THE GREAT TREE

THE BARREN GROUNDS

MISEWA

N
W E
S

SWAMPY CREE GLOSSARY
AND PRONUNCIATION GUIDE

SOUNDS:
É – ay
Í – ee
I – ih
A – ah
O – oh
E – eh

Arikwachas eric-watch-ahs: squirrel
Askí ah-skee: earth, ground
Assini Awasis ah-sin-ih ah-wah-sis: stone child
Atim ah-tim: dog
Ehe eh-heh: yes
Ekosani eh-koh-sah-nih: thank you
Kihiw kih-ewe: eagle
Kisakíhitin kiss-ah-kee-hit-in: I love you
Kiskisitotaso kih-skih-sih-toh-tah-so: don't forget about
    who you are
Kókom koo-kuhm: grandmother
Kokoswak co-coss-wack: pigs
Mahihkan mah-hih-kahn: wolf
Mihko mih-koh: blood
Ministik min-iss-tick: island

Misewa miss-ah-waa: all that is

Miskinahk miss-kih-nack: turtle

Mistapew miss-ta-pay-oh: big foot (giant)

Mwach mwa-ch: no

Muskwa muh-skwa: bear

Nikamon nih-kah-mawn: a song

Níwakomakanak nee-wack-oh-mah-kah-nack: my relatives

Nósisim new-sis-ihm: my grandchild

Ochek oh-check: fisher

Ochekatchakosuk oh-check-ah-chack-oh-suhk: the fisher stars

Oho oh-ho: owl

Otakosík oh-tack-oh-seek: yesterday

Pimíhkán pih-mee-kaan: pemmican

Pisiskowak pih-sis-koh-wack: animals

Tansi tan-sih: hello

ONE

"**E**li, wake up!"

Morgan looked back and forth between her brother and the enormous footprints in the frosted grass that approached the Great Tree and then retreated into the northern woods. Mistapew. She couldn't stop imagining the terrible creature taking Eli's soul and leaving with it. *Why? How?*

"Eli! Wake! Up!"

Morgan had shouted the same three words at least ten times, but Eli hadn't moved in any way, not so much as a flickering eyelid, even when Morgan had tried yelling in his ear. She'd also punched him in the arm, wanting him to tell her to quit it, as he always did. Wanting him to rub his arm as though her punch were harder than it actually was. She wanted him to be faking it, for this to be payback for her going through the portal without him. She wanted him to sit up suddenly and scare the living crap out of her—an elaborate prank, right down to the footprints. Morgan had

1

seen videos where people had faked bigfoot tracks, so how hard could it be?

But with each passing second, it became clear that this was no prank. Her brother would not wake up.

The night before, Morgan had learned that her mother was dead. Feeling lost, wanting to escape, she'd snuck into Eli's room and taken the drawing he'd made of the Barren Grounds. She used it to open the portal and passed through, alone, to find herself at the Great Tree. Eli followed soon after, and, without a word between them, the siblings fell asleep together amidst the thick roots.

At some point during the night, it happened: Mistapew took Eli's soul.

Now Morgan sat down with her back against the tree trunk. The open portal was just above her head (it was a wonder Katie and James hadn't heard her shouting), and Eli's head was in her lap. Why had Mistapew taken Eli's soul and not hers? Had Eli just been closer to where Mistapew came out of the forest? Was it that simple? What other explanation could there be? Was there something special about Eli?

"Why'd you have to sleep by the stupid Great Tree?" Morgan asked herself, banging the back of her head against the rough bark.

She'd heard the story of the eagle Kihiw many times before, from Elders in Misewa, and from Ochek (both as an older fisher but also when they time-traveled and met the animal being when he was younger). By now, she could tell the story herself, and do at least as good a job as young Ochek. People from the village had planned to hunt in the northern woods and, after crossing the Barren Grounds, decided to rest before going any farther. While they were sleeping, Mistapew came into Kihiw's teepee and took his soul. Nobody ever discovered where Mistapew put Kihiw's soul. And because Kihiw could not eat or drink, his body wasted away, and he died.

Immediately after Morgan had recited that last part of the story in her mind, she gasped, looked at her brother, and cradled his head protectively. Eli could not eat or drink either! *He* would waste away and die, unless she did for him what nobody had managed to do for Kihiw.

"I need to find where that giant took your soul," she said to her unresponsive brother.

No medicine could bring Eli back. There was nothing she could force down his mouth, as Mihko had done for her when Muskwa had knocked her out. Nothing that would heal him. She could not yell his name loud enough. She could not punch his arm hard enough.

Morgan scanned the area, desperate for help, but there was nobody around. Of course. She and Eli were between the Barren Grounds and the northern woods. The closest people were actually Katie and James, through the portal and down the stairs on the second floor. But Morgan couldn't ask them for help. They couldn't know about the portal. And besides, James might be a doctor, but what good would a cardiologist be for a person with a stolen soul? She was pretty sure no doctor could treat something like that. No, the help she needed was in Misewa. If somebody knew what to do, if somebody knew where she could start looking for Eli's soul in the northern woods, if somebody even knew what a soul looked like or where it might be kept, it would be an animal being.

Eli needed to be left by the Great Tree, where he'd still be experiencing earth time. Bringing him to Misewa would waste time he didn't have. But she didn't want him left alone there while she went for help, even if, to him, it would seem as though she'd only been gone a few minutes. A lot could happen in two minutes. Had it taken Mistapew more than two minutes to take Eli's soul? Morgan realized she needed someone to sit with him, and, in the end, there was only one person she could think to ask: Emily.

Morgan propped Eli up against the Great Tree, then climbed through the portal into their secret room. She snuck to her bedroom and found her phone, which was still on the floor by her bed, where she'd dropped it. She hesitated a moment, staring at it as the conversation with her kókom played over in her head. Her mother was dead. She'd been worrying so much about Eli that she'd forgotten. But there was no time for sadness now. Morgan did her best to shake off the memory and picked up the phone.

Sneaking back into the secret room, where she could keep an eye on her brother, she dialed Emily's number. It rang once. It rang twice. It rang enough times that Morgan feared Emily wouldn't pick up. But then she did. It was 5:06 a.m.

"Morg, what the heck?" Emily said, half asleep but alert enough to whisper, so as not to wake anybody else in her own home.

"Emily," Morgan said, matching Emily's volume to ensure that Katie and James would also stay asleep. "How fast can you get to my house?"

She rattled off her address and waited while Emily plugged it into her phone so that she could get directions from her house to Morgan's. It felt as though it took forever, and every second mattered.

"Well?" Morgan said.

"Okay, okay, chill out," Emily said. "It'd take me . . . nineteen minutes."

Morgan checked the time: 5:08 a.m. It would take Emily maybe two or three minutes to get ready, nineteen minutes to get there, and another two minutes to sneak up to the attic. That meant when Emily arrived it would be, at worst, 5:32 a.m. Katie and James woke up at 6:00 a.m. Twenty-eight minutes on earth would translate to three days on Askí. Three days to save her brother's life. She couldn't even think about failing, of bringing Eli back to earth the way he was. He'd have to be plugged into machines his whole life, fed through a tube.

"You have to come over," Morgan said.

"You called me at five in the morning to tell me I have to come over after school? I think it could've waited, Morg."

"No, *now*. You have to come over now."

Maybe it was the desperation in Morgan's voice. Maybe it was just that Emily was that good a friend. Whatever the reason, Emily said, "Okay, I'm coming."

"Em, thank you so much. I'll be in the attic."

"In the attic?"

"Yeah, in the attic, to the right, there's a door. Behind the door, there's a room. I'll be in that room." Morgan was talking so fast it must have sounded as if she'd drunk ten cups of coffee. "I'll leave the front door open for you."

"What's this all about?" Emily asked. "What's going on?"

Morgan could hear Emily moving around. She must've been getting changed while she talked. Good. She wasn't wasting time. But how to answer her questions?

"You'll have to see it to believe it," Morgan said.

"A mystery." At Emily's end, Morgan heard a door open and shut; then she heard quick footsteps. Emily was out of the house. "I'll be there soon."

"Emily?"

"Yeah?"

"When you get here, climb the stairs on the *outside* of the steps, not in the middle. They creak in the middle."

"Pro tip. Thanks."

"And Emily?"

"Yeah?"

"Run."

TWO

Fifteen minutes later, Morgan, who'd dizzyingly gone back and forth from Eli's side to the big attic window that faced the street to keep watch for Emily, saw her running towards the house. She'd gotten there four minutes faster than planned. On earth, four minutes was no big deal, but Morgan knew it would give them precious hours on Askí. She hurried across the attic into the secret room and waited there. Ninety seconds later, she heard Emily climb the last flight of stairs before appearing in the doorway. Morgan gave her an enormous hug—for coming, of course, but also because Morgan needed one.

"Whoa," Emily whispered. "I'm happy to see you, too."

"Thank you," Morgan said, her voice muffled by Emily's hooded sweatshirt.

After the hug, Morgan led Emily into the secret room, then took her hands, preparing her for the shock.

"You wanted me to come over this early to . . ." Emily squeezed Morgan's hands. "To propose?"

They smiled at the same time, as if their reactions had been synchronized. Morgan's face felt warm. She let go of Emily's hands and put her hands on her hips, then crossed her arms, then glanced at Emily. Then they looked away from each other. Finally, their eyes met, and they managed to hold each other's gaze.

There was an awkward moment.

"Can you fill me in now?" Emily asked.

"Oh, right." Morgan collected herself. "So, we need to go through here," she said, leading Emily to the portal. Facing it, from their point of view, they could only see the sky. Askí's sky, not earth's sky.

"Onto . . . the roof?" Emily put her hand against the slanted wall the portal was on. "It seems pretty steep to just sit on the roof. Wouldn't we fall off? Do you go through this skylight all the time? How are you not dead?"

"It's not a skylight," Morgan said. "It's a portal."

"A . . ." Emily furrowed her brow. ". . . Portal?"

"Yes. A portal to another world."

"Morgan." For the first time, Emily sounded exasperated with her. Frankly, Morgan was surprised it had taken this long. Over the two weeks of their friendship, all Morgan had been was exasperating. Weird. Detached. Manic—one day sad, another day happy. Emily started towards the door. "You got me up at five in the morning to mess with me? I'm going back to bed."

But Morgan grabbed Emily's hand and pulled her back.

"Wait," she said.

"What?" Emily said. "I'm tired."

"Look *into* it."

"To see your backyard?"

"Just . . . trust me, okay? *Humor* me."

"Fine," Emily said with a big breath out, "and *then* I'm going home."

Emily walked over to the portal. She curled her fingers over the edge, got on her tiptoes, and peered out of the secret room into Askí. As soon as she saw the other world (Morgan knew exactly what Emily saw: the Barren Grounds, the southern woods against the horizon, Misewa), she spun around to face Morgan with a look of confusion and alarm.

"There should be a backyard, and a back lane, and other houses, and the rest of the city," Emily said. She looked again through the portal, then again at Morgan. "What the heck is going on?"

"I told you: it's a portal into another world." Morgan approached the portal and cupped her hands together to give Emily something to step on so that she could climb through. "And we have to go there, like, this minute."

Emily hesitated. "I left a note for my parents, for when they got up, that I was working out in the gym this morning. Like, at school. Not that I was going to another world. How long are we going to be there? Do you know how crazy this is?"

"Yes," Morgan said, "I know how crazy it *seems*. I felt the same way the first time. But time works differently there. If we spend a week on Askí—"

"Askí?"

"That's what the world is called. It literally means 'the world' in Cree. Anyway, if we spend a week there, it'll only be an hour here. My foster parents will be up in,

9

like, half an hour, so we're only going for a few days. Like, three days."

"What?" Emily slapped herself on the cheek. "Am I still dreaming? Can somebody please wake me up?"

Emily was about to slap herself again, but Morgan caught her arm.

"No, you're not dreaming. This is all real." Morgan again made a step with her hands. "Now come on. Eli's in trouble."

It was very likely Morgan's tone, desperate but determined, that stopped Emily from asking any more questions. She nodded, and then used Morgan's hands to climb through the portal. Morgan swiftly followed, entering the portal the way she always did, by grasping the edges of the opening and, bracing her feet against the slanted wall, climbing up and through. On the other side, she found Emily already crouching beside Eli, who was still propped up against the Great Tree. Emily gave him a shake, but he didn't react. She called his name, but he didn't answer.

"What's wrong with him?" she asked.

"Bigfoot took his soul," Morgan said. "And before you say anything, yes, really bigfoot. It's happened before, to an Elder. An eagle named Kihiw."

"Morgan, this is too much. I don't know. I think I'm going to have a panic attack. We're in another reality, there's an Elder eagle, bigfoot, Eli's soul is gone, I . . ."

Morgan got down to eye level with Emily. She put both hands on Emily's shoulders, and her forehead against Emily's forehead.

"I know this is a lot, and I'm sorry for dragging you into this. There'll be more that I have to explain, and I will."

Emily's breathing was fast and shallow. Morgan could feel a cold sweat on her friend's skin. She started to breathe slowly so that Emily would breathe slowly, and after a few seconds she seemed a bit calmer. Or, at least, as calm as one might expect. Morgan felt it was safe to continue.

"For now, I need you to stay here with Eli while I go get help. I need you to keep him safe."

"Okay." Emily still looked to be evening her breath, trying to come to terms with the fact that she'd entered another reality. "I can do that. I can stay with him."

"That village over there." Morgan nodded across the Barren Grounds, where Misewa was visible. "It's where Eli and I stay when we come here. There are beings there who can help us."

"Like . . . beings like regular people?" Emily asked.

"I mean, they're regular to me," Morgan said, "but just so you can prepare yourself, they're animals who walk and talk. But they're *really* nice."

Emily appeared a second away from fainting. "Oh, good. They're nice."

Morgan walked to the edge of where earth's time surrounded the Great Tree.

"I'm going to be back in a minute," Morgan said.

"A minute," Emily repeated, as though she couldn't form words on her own. "Got it."

"Emily, I mean *actually* just one minute. Maybe two."

"I'd say I don't understand, but I think that's a given right now."

"It's like . . . there's a small area around the tree where it's still earth time, but once you go far enough, it's Askí time." Morgan thought back to the first time she and Eli had left Askí, how they'd watched Arik walk a distance from the Great Tree and then suddenly dart off like The Flash. It was weird back then, but Morgan had come to understand that Arik had entered Askí time, where weeks were mere hours on earth. Morgan knew that as soon as she took one step out of the perimeter, Emily would see her zip away in the same manner. What she didn't know was whether she'd explained it well enough, or even if it was explainable at all.

"This'll look odd."

"No kidding," Emily said.

Morgan smiled apologetically at Emily, who'd not asked to be put through any of this, looked worriedly at her brother, then took a calming breath of her own and started to run. She did not look back, keeping her eyes squarely on Misewa.

THREE

Morgan and Eli had now been to the Barren Grounds almost twenty times, and it no longer felt like a big deal to cross it. The journeys across the Barren Grounds in the winter were longer, but although Morgan was running, and it seemed to her that it was late summer or autumn right now, she didn't feel she was getting there any faster. It was as though she were running in slow motion. If only she were really fit, like Emily, who was a hockey player. Look at how fast she'd gotten to Morgan's house! Sure, Morgan had walked countless miles in the North Country, but walking and running were two different things.

What kept her going, especially when her legs started to burn, threatening to give out, was the thought of Eli: he was probably already dangerously dehydrated. While Morgan inched closer to Misewa, she did another sort of calculation. Not Misewa Math. She tried to remember how long the body could survive without water or food.

She'd googled it once, after Ochek had told her that, on the trapline, you ate what you caught, and if you didn't catch anything, you went hungry.

"Well, I'd starve, simple as that," Morgan had said, but then she'd been curious to see how long she might actually survive if she were out on the land by herself. (This was before she'd learned to catch prairie chickens.)

How long does it take to starve to death?

She went deep into the scattered files of her brain and retrieved the information. A person could go thirty or forty days without food. The human body survived that long because it pretty much started eating itself for nutrients.

Thirty or forty days was a long time. If only Eli could drink water, she'd have so much more time to find his soul and figure out a way to get it back into his body. But he could not drink water, and the human body could only go about three days without it. It worked out—Morgan had precisely that many days before Katie and James woke up on earth—but she would much rather have had the thirty or forty days, even if it meant getting caught by Katie and James. As it stood, she'd be going home in mere days with Eli alive or Eli dead. The thought sent a chill across her body.

At long last, Morgan arrived in Misewa, but even then she didn't stop running. She sprinted past longhouses and surprised villagers and headed straight for Arik's dwelling.

Morgan burst into Arik's longhouse shouting, "Arik! Arik! I'm back! Arik!"

She stopped in the middle of the living room beside the fire, which was burning bright, and looked around anxiously. It was just as it had been when Ochek lived there, except for the collection of Eli's pictures Arik had hung up all over the walls. She hadn't made any other changes while Morgan and Eli had been absent, all the time they'd been gone while traveling to the past. But where was Arik? Morgan knew she wasn't out on the land, because the fire was burning.

"Arik?"

She heard rustling in the other room, then soft footsteps. She saw Arik's sharp fingertips appear first, curling around the edge of the doorway, then her ears slowly inching into view, and finally, Arik stepped into the living room, beaming.

"Morgan!" she cried. "I could hardly believe it was you when I heard your voice! It's been so long!"

Arik rushed over and gave Morgan not a squirrel hug but a bear hug, and Morgan got so caught up in it—she was so happy to see her old friend—that she forgot why she'd rushed there in the first place.

"Where on Askí have you been?" Arik asked.

Morgan looked fondly at the animal being. Even though she and Eli had been with Arik's younger self just two days ago, it had been a while since they had seen present-day Arik.

"I was here," Morgan said, "just . . . not now."

Arik ended the hug and held Morgan at arm's length. She didn't need to say anything; her facial expression alone demanded further explanation.

"Do you remember, before the White Time came, when we were here? You were living in Otakosík, the Great Bear destroyed it, and you fought with us against—"

"Yes, yes, I remember that," Arik said. "I also remember that I was never supposed to speak of it. You were never supposed to know that you'd been to the North Country before."

"I know you weren't supposed to tell us," Morgan said, "but it's not a secret anymore. Remember when we were leaving? When Eli and I told you and Ochek we were going to come back one day so we could save Misewa together?"

Arik nodded.

"I literally just did that yesterday."

"No way!" Arik gasped.

"Yes way! Crazy, right?"

"So crazy! Nuts even, and not the kind I like to eat!"

Morgan laughed, then hugged Arik all over again.

"Oh, I've missed you so much!"

She rubbed her hand against the fur on the back of Arik's neck. They kept hugging until everything from the last day pushed into her brain.

"Eli!" Morgan said, breaking off the hug.

"What about him?" Arik said. "How awful of me that I didn't even notice he wasn't with you! I've missed him just as much!"

"He's back at the Great Tree!"

"What? Why? Afraid I'd be mad that you two were gone for so long, I bet. He's a sensitive one, that boy."

"No, that's not it at all! We fell asleep at the tree and . . . and . . ." Morgan finished speaking through tears and heaving breaths, ". . . Mistapew took his soul!"

Morgan recounted the entire story to Arik, every sad detail, leaving out only what had led her to go through the portal and do something as reckless as sleep on the roots of the Great Tree: finding out that her mother had died. She didn't feel ready to talk about that, and in any case there was not enough time to discuss it, even if she'd wanted to. So Morgan skipped that part and, to finish, explained that Emily, a human the village could trust, was watching over Eli right now.

"I need to save him, Arik. There has to be a way to save him."

"I—"

"You *have* to know a way. You're so old, you know so much."

"Dear one," Arik said, "I will help you in any way that I can. I will follow you to the ends of Askí to save your brother. But I . . ." She let out a deep sigh. "All my years have taught me nothing about this. There's only one thing I can think to do."

Minutes later, Arik and Morgan were sitting across the fire from Muskwa, Oho, and Miskinahk in the Council Hut. While they smudged to prepare for the meeting, Morgan couldn't help but stare at Muskwa and think about the adventure they'd just gone on. She looked back and forth, from the Great Bear's scar to his kind, wizened face. She knew how he'd come by the scar now, about the vicious slash he'd received from Pip's sword. Pip, the warrior bird. And, of course, she knew that *he* knew she'd been involved with his defeat when he'd tried to ransack Misewa so many years earlier. All the time travel stuff was confusing, but it made things clear for Morgan. It made her understand why Muskwa had trusted her and Eli to go with Ochek and Arik to find the summer birds on their first visit, why he'd invited them to stay in Misewa, why he'd said that they would always be welcome in the village.

After Muskwa had pulled smoke from the smudge bowl over his body, heart, mouth, eyes, and head, he placed the bowl on the ground and the meeting began. Arik had explained what was going on while calling the leaders of the community together, but with only the barest of details. So, to start things off, Morgan was invited to recount what had happened in her own words. Morgan tried to speak calmly, to be certain she gave them all the information she could, so that, as soon as possible, they could figure out how to save Eli. But it became apparent to her that they were just as much at a loss as she was. Worse, she could see in their faces that they thought nothing could be done.

Morgan felt her heart breaking inside her chest.

"When Kihiw had his soul taken, he was given every possible medicine that could be given," Miskinahk, the turtle, said.

"Only those that could be applied to his body, in the end," Oho, the owl, said, "because he could not be made to swallow."

"Even still," Muskwa said, staring hopelessly at the smoke rising from the smudge bowl, "what medicine can summon a soul back into the body? It wouldn't have mattered."

There were a few seconds of silence before Muskwa roared and threw the smudge bowl across the hut. It hit the side of the structure—right over the ocher painting that documented the journey Morgan, Eli, Arik, and Ochek had gone on to find the summer birds—and shattered into hundreds of pieces. Morgan jumped to her feet at Muskwa's outburst, and then she stared at the fragments of the smudge bowl, just as Muskwa had stared at the smoke. She thought, *That's what my heart looks like right now.*

"You've all just given up on him already, haven't you?" Morgan whispered, still staring at the smudge bowl.

"We aren't giving up. There's simply nothing we can do," Miskinahk said. "If there were anything, any answer at all, Kihiw would have survived."

"We're sorry," Oho said. "We truly are."

Arik reached for Morgan's hand to comfort her, as though Eli were already gone, as though it were all over but the waiting. She thought of Emily sitting at the Great Tree, Eli resting against her. She thought of Eli, and his unwavering love and faith for the village and all the animal beings within it. As soon as Arik's paw touched Morgan's skin, she snatched her hand away.

"How dare you?" she shouted, even louder than Muskwa's roar. "Eli would never give up on you! He never has! How dare all of you? You're telling me, to my face, that nothing can be done because your Elder eagle would have lived? You're telling me that you put some ointment on his feathers and then you just gave up? You were all like, 'Okay, we're done here, let's call it a night!' No! I don't believe it! You don't know what to do because you never did anything! You never tried! Now you're just going to let my brother die because of it?"

"Morgan," Muskwa said. "You know that we don't want that. You know that we would do whatever we could. You and your brother are one of us. Níwakomakanak. My relatives."

"Don't you níwakomakanak me, Muskwa!" Morgan pointed a finger at Muskwa and all the Council members, then she stormed off to the edge of the hut. Her feet crunched over the fragments of the smudge bowl.

After a minute of silence, of just staring at the wall, Morgan spoke. "Ochek told me and Eli the story of Kihiw, you know," she said quietly, "when we were on our way to get the summer birds. The story of Mistapew, and how he steals souls. 'Like a ghost,' Ochek said. That's how he must've come to take Eli's soul. Like a ghost." She walked back over to the fire, then around it so that she was standing right in front of Muskwa. "What I remember most about the story is that Eli asked Ochek if anybody had ever looked for Kihiw's soul. And do you know what Ochek said?" She waited for an answer. She looked at each one of the leadership group. At Miskinahk. At Oho. And finally, at Muskwa. There came no answer. "He said, 'No.'" She leaned in closer, so that her nose was almost touching his nose. "So how can you tell me," she hissed, "that there's nothing we can do when you never tried?"

"He warned us never to return," Muskwa said. "He warned us never to enter the northern woods."

"Well, guess what?" Morgan walked to the hut's flap. There, she stopped. "If that's where Mistapew took Eli's soul, then that's where I'm going to go." She looked at Arik. "Are you with me?"

Arik stood up and joined Morgan at the entrance.

"I told you," she said. "To the ends of Askí."

"You don't know how dangerous the northern woods are," Miskinahk said.

"Muskwa, you must stop her," Oho pleaded.

But Muskwa, after locking eyes with a determined Morgan, shook his head. "Mwach, I will not stop her." He got to his feet with some effort, getting on in age as he was, and approached Morgan.

"Good," Morgan said. "Because I just lost somebody, and I'm not going to lose somebody else."

The Great Bear placed a tobacco tie on Morgan's palm. "May Creator keep you safe."

"Somebody's got to, right?"

Morgan left the hut with Arik trailing behind her. Emily was waiting for her, and somewhere in the northern woods, so was Eli's soul.

FOUR

Morgan and Arik packed hurriedly—materials to build a tent, enough pimíhkán to last a few days in case they failed to catch any game (if there was any game at all—some in the village believed the northern woods were devoid of any life), a pot to boil water for tea or to add to the pimíhkán for stew (they brought some flour for that purpose as well), tools, and weapons: a Bo staff for Arik, Morgan's trusty slingshot (the one she'd killed the prairie chicken with), and a hatchet for Emily. Emily seemed like a hatchet kind of person to Morgan. She was tough like that—Ochek kind of tough. Finally, they borrowed one of the sleds in the village that was used to haul large game— caribou or moose . . . or, in this case, a twelve-year-old boy.

Once ready, they wasted no time and were seen off by a handful of nervous villagers—including Chief and Council—as they entered the Barren Grounds, with the northern woods looming on the horizon. By then, Morgan had been in Misewa for about two hours. She'd run there in twenty minutes and estimated it would take twice as long to walk back. That was three hours total. She did a quick Misewa Math calculation in her head. *If one week is one hour, that means one day is about eight and a half minutes. Half a day is four minutes and fifteen seconds. Six hours is two minutes and seven seconds, give or take. Three hours is one minute and, like, three and a half seconds.* It was rough, she didn't have a calculator, but it meant that Emily would only have been waiting a little over a minute.

"There are some things about this place that are still crazy to me, even after all this time," Morgan said aloud after going over her basic equation.

"Like how you time traveled?" Arik asked.

"Yeah, *that*, of course. But I've been rushing around trying to get things sorted out here—"

"With *my* help."

"With *your* help," Morgan corrected herself, "and in the end, do you know how long my friend will have been waiting for me?"

"How long?"

"Like one minute. Sixty seconds."

"Not to sound defensive, Morgan, but have you considered that there are some things about earth, even though I've only seen the attic of earth, that seem crazy to me? Put the moccasin on the other foot, dear girl. I waited for you for over two turns of the seasons, and I bet it was nothing to you."

"It was *not* nothing to me," Morgan said.

"Here I was, pining for my missing human friends," Arik put the back of her paw against her forehead dramatically, "going to the Great Tree and waiting for you for hours on end, every day, every week, and you were off getting to know the younger me the whole time."

"*Younger* you?" Morgan teased.

"I *was* younger back then, you know. I age. I just age slowly."

"I know. I'm just teasing you."

They'd been walking for half an hour now. Morgan had been pulling the empty sled the whole time, so they switched, because her hands were getting sore. She couldn't imagine what it was going to be like with Eli on the sled. It would make the load at least twice as heavy, as small as her brother was for his age. Plus, they wouldn't be going over flat lands like the Barren Grounds, they'd be traversing a forest. Not ideal terrain. With Arik pulling the sled, they kept talking as though they'd not stopped.

"I can't believe the whole time we were here, the first time Eli and I came, you never let on that we'd been here years before," Morgan said.

"You told Ochek and me not to say a word to you about that, so . . ." Arik mimed zipping her mouth shut.

"Didn't you want to? I mean, weren't you excited?"

"Of course I was excited! I'd had such a fun time with you two back then. Even when we almost got killed by Muskwa, it was so much fun."

"It was not at all fun fighting with Muskwa."

"Yes, well," Arik said, "everything but that."

"I'm amazed Ochek kept the secret, too," Morgan said. "Ochek especially. Like, you're *you* all the time, always in the best mood. I don't think keeping a secret made any difference to how you acted. But Ochek must have had to work so hard to keep that poker face he had going." Morgan smiled and shook her head at the memory of Ochek in the first days after she and Eli had met him. "All grumpy and everything."

"In his defense, he'd been pretty hardened by then. The years we all spent in the White Time were difficult."

"Were the other villagers acting, too? Wow, if they were, they all deserve Academy Awards! Remember when they . . ." She didn't finish the sentence, and she didn't have to. Morgan was remembering getting yelled at, having things thrown at them while they were on their way to the Council Hut. But Arik had been with them, after all. She'd seen snowballs hurtling towards Morgan and Eli. She'd heard the animal beings yelling at the siblings, the beaver slapping its tail.

"At the time, they didn't know you would return," Arik explained. "Ochek and I kept your secret very well. I'm sure they recognized you, and they were surprised to see you both after all those years. But . . ." Arik stopped. Her face read as though she was apologizing for the entire village. "They were angry, Morgan. And bitter. And hungry. And dying. Just days after you left, Mason wandered into the village. It seemed maybe he'd be as nice as you and Eli had been, but then . . . he did what he did. I think, at first, they blamed you for it."

"They should've!" Morgan said. "We were the ones who let him into the North Country."

"You couldn't have known Mason was going to come to Misewa, and you couldn't have known he was going to steal the summer birds." Arik started walking again. "It took them a little while to see that you were not like him, and that it wasn't your fault. You're accountable for your own actions, and your actions have always been good. Mason's accountable for what he did, too."

"He kind of paid for it, didn't he?"

"Yes, he kind of did," Arik said, "thanks to Mahihkan."

Emily was still at the Great Tree when Morgan and Arik arrived. Eli was cradled in her arms, leaning against her.

"She's a little freaked out, just to give you a heads-up," Morgan said.

"Naturally," Arik said. "Who wouldn't be? She's in a new world, Eli's soul is not in his body . . ."

Arik may have intended to go on, but when they stopped at the perimeter and she noticed Eli, she put her paw against her chest, right over her heart. Her head tilted to one side, and she breathed out as though she was trying to stop herself from crying, a quavering breath. But Morgan saw the tears, and if Arik had been trying to stop them before, she didn't wipe them away now. Morgan remembered something Muskwa had told her once. *A tear is your body letting out the pain.* Arik must have been in as much pain as Morgan was.

"Oh, my poor boy. My dear, sweet Eli. What has that thing done to him?"

Arik went right to Eli, giving Emily a simple head nod, so focused on Eli was she. Arik eased Eli off Emily's lap and onto her own, and she held him, wrapped her arms tightly around him as though his soul were not gone yet, as though she were trying to hold it in. Morgan sat on the ground beside Emily and put an arm around her.

"Are you okay?" Morgan asked.

"Yeah," Emily said, staring at Arik. "Yeah, I'm fine. I was, you know, mentally preparing for this. I could've maybe done with a bit more time, though."

"I know. I'm sorry. I'm sorry for throwing this all on you. I just . . . I needed you."

Emily held Morgan's hand reassuringly. "I'm glad you called me. I'm glad you needed me. I just have to get used to all this."

"It'd probably be a good start to introduce you to Arik," Morgan said. "Arik is short for Arikwachas, which means squirrel in Cree. But she likes to be called Arik."

"She's a squirrel, but she's tall and walks upright like a person, and wears clothes?" Emily said.

"She does, yep. All of that. Except she's not tall. Tall for a regular squirrel, but, you know, kind of short compared to me and you."

"So she's a squirrel, but she's tall—"

"For a regular squirrel."

"Right, okay, she's tall for a regular squirrel," Emily said, "walks upright like a regular *person*, and wears clothes?"

"That's about right," Morgan said.

"And she talks," Emily said.

Arik looked up from Eli and, through her tears, managed to grin at Emily and Morgan. "I'm sitting right here, you know."

"Also true," Morgan said. "She talks. A lot. Usually."

"Hey," Arik said.

"Well, you do."

Emily took a deep breath. "I'm Emily. Emily Houldsworth."

"It's nice to meet you, Emily," Arik said. "I wish it were under better circumstances."

"Yeah, me too."

Arik stroked Eli's hair, and soothed him as though he were only sleeping. Emily and Morgan watched. Morgan's heart was already broken. Now it was being ground into powder, as though it were being made into pimíhkán. She was sure Emily's heart was breaking too. Morgan had never seen Arik like this. There were no jokes. There was no silliness. There was no joy; the squirrel being's grin was just a spark. As Arik's soothing turned into a song that was too quiet for the girls to hear, a song that was meant only for Eli, Morgan saw sadness in her. Arik's paw was shaking as she ran her fingers through Eli's hair. Morgan put her head on Emily's shoulder. Emily squeezed Morgan's hand tighter, then kissed her on the top of her head. For a short while, that's how they stayed. The girls comforting each other, Arik caring for Eli. But Morgan knew that they needed to start moving, so she cleared her throat and lifted her head.

"What do we do now?" she asked. "Where do we go?"

"We go into the northern woods, and we don't stop looking until we've looked everywhere," Arik said.

"Sorry if you guys know this already, but do you have any idea what a soul actually looks like?" Emily asked.

"Not exactly," Arik said, "but I suppose we'll know it when we see it."

"It'll probably be glowing or something, right?" Morgan posited, thinking of ghost videos and pictures she'd seen on the internet. "Like maybe he'll be an orb of light, or a translucent figure that's glowing, like, a moon-type color?"

Emily looked into the dark and unwelcoming northern woods. "I guess if his soul's glowing, it won't be hard to find in there."

"However it might appear, we'll look in every bush, behind every tree, under every stone," Arik said.

Arik's determination was catching. Morgan got to her feet. Emily did, too. All three of them lifted Eli up and placed him gently on the sled. Arik had prepared it with hide so that it was soft for him. It made the load heavier, but no matter.

"Would Mistapew really put a soul in a bush or behind a tree or under a stone?" Morgan asked. "There has to be something else. It seems to me that you'd put a soul someplace special. At least *I* would."

"We need to find bigfoot," Emily said. "I mean, he's the only one who'll know where Eli's soul is, right?"

"Emily is right," Arik said. "We need to find Mistapew. If we find Mistapew, we'll find Eli's soul."

"Okay, yeah," Morgan said, "but we're still left needing to find something. He walks around all over the place, doesn't he?"

"We've got to find his home," Emily said. "Everybody has a home."

"Morgan, you've brought a very smart friend with you," Arik said.

Morgan looked at Emily affectionately. "Yes, I have."

Emily's idea to look for Mistapew's dwelling, whatever that might be—a cabin (unlikely), a wigwam (the biggest wigwam ever constructed), a den (Morgan figured this was most likely)—was a good one. They set off at once, and since Morgan and Arik had taken turns hauling the sled across the Barren Grounds, Emily volunteered to start off pulling Eli through the northern woods. Arik, and Morgan, who'd developed blisters from the work, readily agreed.

"You've got brains *and* brawn," Morgan told Emily.

Emily picked up the rope and secured it around her hips for some extra support, something neither Morgan nor Arik had thought of. Another checkmark in the "Emily's Smart" column.

"Don't forget beauty," Emily said.

"Yeah," Morgan said, "you've got all the words that start with *B*."

"Except the bad ones."

"Right. None of the bad ones, all the good ones."

Morgan winked at Emily, and immediately felt stupid because that was something only grandparents did. As usual, however, Emily didn't make her feel dumb. She just winked back exaggeratedly.

The three travelers, with their unconscious cargo, left the Great Tree and faced the threshold of the northern woods.

"To boldly go where no man has gone before," Morgan said under her breath.

"A *Star Trek* reference? Really?" Emily said. "Yuck."

"I know. I instantly felt bad about saying that. It feels like cheating on Star Wars."

"That's because it *is* like cheating on Star Wars."

"No beings at all have gone here before," Arik said. "Not for many, many years, at least. Too many years to count."

From the edge of the northern woods, the path ahead looked intimidating. Morgan hadn't taken a long look into the forest since being told the story about Mistapew and Kihiw, as though if she stared too long the giant might come running at her. The northern woods were dark, even in the midday sun. The tree canopy was thick overhead and blotted out the light, which broke through only sporadically in tiny shafts. A sharp wind sounded like distant, howling wolves and was cool against Morgan's skin.

There was a smell of death.

The suggestion of a path from the Great Tree into the woods encouraged a direction to start. What else would have made it other than the giant? Maybe following it would lead them where they needed to go.

After that, well, they'd just have to figure it out.

FIVE

The temperature dropped quickly. Morgan had permanent goose pimples all over her body, but she wasn't sure if it was from the chill or how unsettling the northern woods were. The trees, thick and tall and ancient, had branches that were bare below but gathered leaves in ever-bigger clusters the closer they reached to the sky, as though they were desperate for any sort of warmth, any sort of light, any sort of life. Those lower branches, reaching out like crooked bones, were caked in spiderwebs. The webs connected twigs and branches and stretched from tree to tree. The only time the northern woods looked kind of pretty was when a beam of sunlight filtered through the webs and lit them up like veins of light, as though to prove, despite how dead the trees looked, that they were really alive. Everything in the North Country was vibrant with earthy tones—blue and brown and green burst out from the sky, from mother earth, and from all that was between. From everything, that is, but the northern woods. There didn't seem to be any colors except high up above. The trees, the bush, the path they were following, all were splashed with shades of gray.

"It's like we're in a galaxy far, far away from Askí," Morgan said.

"Dude, you already cheated on Star Wars and you can't make up for it now," Emily said.

She was still pulling the sled, and sweat beaded on her forehead. It looked just as hard as Morgan thought it would be, navigating the wooden vehicle over the uneven landscape. Somebody else would have to take a turn soon.

"I figured." Morgan said. "But it does feel like that."

"Are we not, quite possibly, if you think about it, really in a galaxy far, far away?" Arik asked. "I mean, not for me, but for you two."

"I've always thought that we're either in another reality that's, like, somehow existing in the same place as earth," Morgan said, "or that we're somewhere across the universe. I don't think we'll ever really know. And then there's the time thing, like . . ." Morgan acted out her head exploding, moving her hands away from her head while spreading her fingers out.

"You'd have to get a scientist over here to study that," Emily said.

"No!" Morgan said. "Nobody else is finding out about Askí. Not from earth. Not if I have anything to say about it."

"Whoa," Emily said. "Relax."

"Sorry," Morgan said. "It's just . . . I've got a lot to fill you in about. We've lived here for a long time and some bad stuff has happened. The worst was with a super crappy guy named Mason."

"Alright, no scientists. Not all mysteries need to be solved," Emily said. "Just look at *Unsolved Mysteries.*"

"That's a television show on earth," Morgan said, anticipating Arik's confusion.

"Look at all the things I learn when you decide to visit," Arik said.

"Don't be bitter about that anymore, please," Morgan said. "If I hadn't gone to the past . . ."

"I know, I know," Arik said. "I just missed you."

"Gone to the past?" Emily said.

"That's *another* story," Morgan said.

"Ah," Emily said. "So many stories are coming my way."

They walked farther into the northern woods, and as they did, Morgan did share stories with Emily, because there was nothing more to do than walk and talk as they continued on the path. She told her friend about their first trip to Askí, in the dead of a never-ending winter, about Ochek, the villagers, Arik, and their perilous journey over the mountain and back again to save, then release, the summer birds. She told her about the sacrifice Ochek had made to set the birds free, about how the grizzled hunter had softened in the precious weeks they'd known him. She pointed towards the sky, to roughly where Ochekatchakosuk would have been if it were night and the trees weren't blotting out the sky. She told her about their journey to the past, how they met Ochek as a teenager, and how wonderful it was to see him again, to have time with him that they never thought they'd have. She told her that it was a chance to have a goodbye that lasted weeks, and that sometimes you don't get a chance to say goodbye at all. She told her all about the first and last trips she and Eli had made to Misewa, and all the times in between, and as Morgan told her stories, it grew progressively darker.

This made a quick flash of yellow near the brush underfoot more pronounced. Morgan saw it out of the corner of her eye, but when she didn't see it again, she brushed it off. If the giant had yellow eyes, they wouldn't be that close to the ground. His eyes would be somewhere where the leaves started, Morgan figured. She didn't actually know how big Mistapew was, and when she'd asked Arik, she'd admitted she didn't know either. Nobody in Misewa had seen him.

Not long after, Morgan saw the yellow for a second time.

"Okay, please tell me that somebody else is seeing that!" she said excitedly.

"Seeing what?" Emily said, scanning the forest from side to side.

"There's really not much to see here, Morgan. Just dead trees and brush and darkness," Arik said. "It's boring, to be perfectly honest."

"There's this, like, yellow light over there," Morgan said, pointing to where she'd seen it. "It was there two times, like a lightning strike. Like, *pow*, and then it was gone."

Arik shrugged.

Emily looked apologetic. "Maybe it's the sun glinting off something."

"I know what I saw," Morgan said. "It was like two little beams of yellow. I saw it *twice*. We're being followed."

"Do you think you might be a bit on edge?" Arik said. "After all, you've been through a lot lately, haven't you?"

"I'm proud you're keeping it together," Emily said. "You're doing better than I was."

"Going through something doesn't make you see yellow lights," Morgan said. "It makes you cry, it makes you sad, it makes your nerves act all crazy, but it does *not* make you see yellow lights."

"Okay, okay," Emily said. "I believe you, but it really could be anything."

"I believe you, too," Arik said. "You've not led me wrong before. I apologize. Let's just keep our eyes open and our ears perked. It shouldn't be hard to miss if we're looking."

The group kept their eyes peeled after that. They continually surveyed the area as they took steps deeper into the forest. But as time passed, the yellow, whether sunlight glinting off something shiny or a set of wicked eyes, did not present itself again. And with each passing second, Morgan began to wonder if she'd seen anything at all. They'd only been flashes, that was that. Maybe it *had* been stress, and who would have blamed her for it? Not Emily and Arik. Morgan kept her doubts to herself and continued to look, fruitlessly, like the other two.

They went farther into the northern woods, feeling more and more as though they were in a place that hadn't been walked in for many years, that perhaps hadn't been walked in at all. Ever. Not by anybody or anything but Mistapew, because as deep as they went, that one path remained. They'd not strayed from it because they couldn't think of another direction to go in, and frankly they were too nervous. The path felt like a safety blanket in this strange forest.

The sled switched from one set of hands to another, then another, rotating through the group. Morgan took it from Emily first, and when she grew tired, Arik took it from Morgan. Being the oldest and smallest of the three, Arik held it the shortest amount of time, before Emily assumed the job of pulling it once again. Day turned into night, and they stopped only once to make torches out of dried wood. Torchlight made the northern woods even scarier, the low light casting long shadows like a crowd of black ghosts floating above the ground.

But in all this time, there was still no yellow.

SIX

Eventually, though the group did not lose their resolve, they *did* lose most of their energy. They'd been walking the whole day, and decided it was best to have supper and rest for the night. In the morning, with two days left to find Eli's soul, they would set off early.

The torches were used to make a large fire, in the hope that if there were any predators, it would keep them at bay. After the fire got going, they prepared the camp. Morgan made a spit, on which they'd hang a pot to boil water for the stew, and Emily helped Arik put the tent up.

When she'd finished the spit, Morgan moved Eli close to the fire to keep his body warm. She'd noticed that he was shaking, his lips were quivering, but that stopped once he was warmed by the flames. When everything was finished, they sat around the fire with their stew, glad to be eating and resting, but still somber because they had nothing to show for the day's efforts but sore feet and legs.

"I'll take the first watch," Arik offered. "I don't sleep much anyway."

"Okay, but don't you just let us sleep through the night," Morgan warned. "I know you'd try to do that. You need to rest, too."

"You two are like grandma and granddaughter," Emily said. "It's weird and comforting and cute all at the same time."

"Grandma? Just grandma?" Arik said, sounding offended. "I'll have you know, young lady, that I'm old enough to be Morgan's great-great-great-great-great—"

"And yet you're mature enough to be my little sister," Morgan said, and at that, laughter pushed the despondency away for a moment.

Arik said that if she saw Mistapew approach the camp-site, she would wake the girls up quickly, and whoever else was keeping watch should do the same. For all Arik knew, the giant was only interested in stealing souls, and to have your soul taken you had to be dreaming. If you were awake, your soul was safe.

"*That's* why he sneaks around like the boogeyman," Emily said.

"Why is that?" Morgan asked. "Why do you have to be dreaming?"

"Dreams are powerful," Arik said. "Dreams help us make sense of the world in ways that we can't while we're awake. They help us to connect with our lives."

Morgan thought of the recurring dream she'd had of her mother.

"Dreams are a way of knowing," Arik continued, "beyond what you call science or math. We need to listen to them, and things can be revealed to us that we wouldn't otherwise be able to understand. They are a connection to the spirit world, and so, when we are dreaming, our spirits are most exposed."

"That makes sense," Morgan said. "I mean, I know dreams are important to me, but I've never thought they were *that* important." The next time she dreamed of her mother, she decided that she would listen more carefully, work to remember more of what happened, feel everything she could, to see what, if anything, her mother was trying to reveal to her.

"On that note, I've been pulling the sled way more than you guys . . . which I'm only stating as a fact. I'm not complaining about it," Emily said. "I think I'm going to turn in for the night."

"I'll be right there," Morgan said.

Emily put her bowl on the ground, thanked Arik for the meal, and then stood up. She clapped some debris off her hands, and some dirt off her pants, and started towards the tent.

"You're going to be okay out here?" Morgan asked Arik. "*Grandma?*"

"Yes. I think it's kind of peaceful, actually," Arik said. "And you can shut your lips about the grandma thing, unless you're going to call me great, too."

"You *are* great. You know, on earth, people want to be thought of as younger, not older."

"Why?" Arik seemed genuinely taken aback. "Age is wisdom, experience, and knowledge. I would never want to be thought of as younger."

"Trust me, I know," Morgan said. "You always make sure to talk about how old you are."

"Hey, guys?" Emily said.

Morgan hadn't noticed, but Emily hadn't gone into the tent. She was standing outside the flap, staring at the ground beneath her feet. Her arms were out, as though she was trying to keep her balance.

"What's wrong?" Morgan asked.

"Something just moved . . . under the ground," Emily said.

"Creator be praised," Arik said, "there is life in the northern woods after all. Maybe it was a rodent of some kind. Maybe we'll catch it and be able to eat something other than—"

"No, it was *under* the ground. It moved like it was swimming in water."

"I think this is where I say that it's been a stressful day, you've just gone to another reality, met an animal being that walks and talks, and you're probably imagining it," Morgan said.

"I don't know you well enough to say that you've never led me wrong," Arik said, "so Morgan might have a point."

"No, I'm telling you, I saw it and I felt it," Emily said. "It was right there, and then it went deeper into the ground or something. It disappeared."

"Maybe it was a gopher," Morgan said.

"Gophers dig under the ground, they don't swim through it," Emily said.

"Okay, look, I—"

"There!" Emily jumped back, almost falling on the tent and knocking it to the ground. She pointed at the base of a tree. "It looked like a big root, and then it broke off. They're all over, Morg. Come here."

"Hang on." Morgan was still not convinced, especially because nobody had believed her about the yellow things. All that being said, she found it hard to disbelieve her friend, so she got up and walked over to Emily, who was now leaning against the tent as though she might yet fall into it. Morgan eased her back into standing straight. "Okay, show me."

"Watch," Emily said.

Arik joined them, and they were all standing in front of the tent, staring intently at the ground for any sign of movement. It was dead silent, darker away from the fire, which made the ground hard to see clearly, and they stared for long minutes until Morgan finally saw it. What looked like part of a root broke off and, yes, it looked to be swimming underground. It came towards them, which made Morgan lift her feet up as though she were dodging a mouse as it moved past.

"Holy crap," Morgan said. "What are these things?"

"I've never seen anything like it before," Arik said.

"On second thought, I'll take the first watch," Emily said. "There's no way I'm sleeping in the tent, on the ground, when there are things swimming through the earth. I'll take *all* the watches."

"You don't have to stay up all night," Morgan said. "I'm sure they're harmless. They're like, I don't know, little logs. They're creepy, but that's just because we've never seen them before."

"Bats are creepy until you get to know them," Arik offered. "Hanging upside down to sleep and whatnot."

"Yeah, they're just new, Houldsy," Morgan said, agreeing with Arik to encourage Emily to calm down. "Just because they're creepy right now doesn't mean they're, like, monsters or something."

Emily breathed in through her nose with her eyes closed, and then let the air out of her mouth slowly. She opened her eyes. "You're right. We can just maybe stack up the hides so we won't feel the things underneath us and it'll be okay. Right?"

"Right," Morgan said. "Nothing bad is going to hap—"

At that moment, there was a shriek like a banshee's that echoed through the woods. Immediately after the awful sound, one of the creatures burst from the ground like a geyser. It had been swimming through the dirt; now it seemed as though it could fly through the air. And it was coming right towards them. In the firelight, as it hurtled ever closer, Morgan could see its face. It had blood-red eyes with thick black pupils, and a snout shaped like a cone that opened wider than Morgan could believe, baring razor-sharp teeth and a tongue that looked like a miniature plunger. Green saliva inside its mouth looked like webbing.

It shrieked again.

The girls screamed.

A large shadow jumped into the air and grabbed the creature right before it bit Emily. The dark figure landed on the other side of the fire, then rolled out of sight. There was a different kind of shriek, this one sounding like agony.

The shriek was followed by growling, and then everything was quiet again.

Morgan, Emily, and Arik were frozen in place, watching the spot where the figure had gone out of sight. They were peering into the darkness. Even with the fire raging it looked blacker than midnight, until a set of yellow eyes appeared.

"That's them! The yellow eyes!" Morgan said. "I told you!"

The yellow eyes got bigger, the shadow got closer, until firelight hit the figure, revealing who it was. Morgan felt like she couldn't breathe. This wasn't real. Walking around the fire, towards them, was Mahihkan. The wolf that had once tried to kill her and Eli and Ochek and Arik, then ended up saving their lives. He was wearing tattered black pants and a ripped black vest. There were scars all over his body where fur refused to grow anymore. He looked beaten and weathered.

"How . . . what . . ." Morgan started.

"Those things are attracted to warmth and heavy movements," Mahihkan said, ignoring Morgan's shock, "and there'll be more of them. If you have weapons, I'd fetch them now."

It was only then that he looked at Morgan, and nodded.

"Tansi. It's good to see you again."

SEVEN

Mahihkan stood protectively between Eli and the woods in a fighting stance, claws out. For now, Morgan put aside questions of how the wolf had survived the canyon fall, why he was in the northern woods, and where he'd been the last seven years. She and the others hurried to get their weapons. Arik grabbed her Bo staff, Emily the hatchet, and Morgan dug out her slingshot. But when she had the slingshot in hand, she wondered how effective it would be against the creatures. They weren't prairie chickens, that was for sure, and her aim wasn't good enough to knock them out of midair. There weren't even any suitable stones on the ground to use as ammunition. What would she shoot? Dirt? Morgan dropped her slingshot and made a quick decision to use a piece of burning wood from the fire, a weapon that had worked for her in the past.

By the time Morgan had retrieved a suitable piece of wood, one that was half burning and half not, Arik and Emily were already with Mahihkan. When Morgan joined the group, they formed a protective barrier around Eli. All sides were covered, by either Mahihkan, Emily, Arik, Morgan, or the towering flames.

Now they were prepared against another strike, but the forest was unmoving, and there was no sound but the crackling and snapping of the bonfire. Morgan waved her torch back and forth, trying to see into the woods or to spot one of the creatures swimming underground, but she couldn't see anything.

"I've got a bad feeling about this," Emily said.

"It's way too quiet," Arik agreed.

"In every story, like, ever, when somebody says, 'It's way too quiet,' that means something awful's about to happen," Morgan said.

"So I shouldn't have said that?"

"Quiet, all of you," Mahihkan said. "If you're talking, you're distracted. You can't be distracted against the groundlings."

"Groundlings?" Morgan said. "Who would give those things such a cute name?"

"*I* named them that."

"Okay. Why would *you* ever give those things such a cute name?"

"I just did," Mahihkan said defensively. "They're small and they move underground. Groundlings."

Morgan shrugged in acceptance. She waved the torch from side to side again, and saw only the dead forest. She walked to the other side of Eli, doing the same thing, and then back to where she'd started.

Nothing.

"Just be still," Mahihkan said. "If you are quiet and still, you can feel them coming before they scream. If you only hear the scream, it may be too late."

"Okay, that's horrifying," Emily said.

It was enough to halt the conversation. There was not a sound. Even the fire seemed to crackle in whispers. That's when Morgan felt tiny tremors on the soles of her moccasins, which were worn down, with a hole in one of them where the ball of her foot touched the ground, dirt against skin.

"Can you feel that?" Morgan asked.

"Yes," Mahihkan said. "They're coming."

"Oh god," Emily said.

"Creator give us strength," Arik said.

"Be ready," Mahihkan said.

All four of them raised their weapons and stared into the dark. The tremors now felt like a distant earthquake. Morgan looked down to see particles of dirt dancing across the ground. As soon as she'd turned her attention away from the forest, there came shrieks. Not just one, like before. This time, the shrieking came from all sides. Out of the darkness came the groundlings, hurtling through the air towards them, their white teeth blinding in the firelight, their red eyes burning brighter than the flames, their tongues pulsing inside their mouths.

There were two coming at Morgan. She grabbed her torch with both hands and swung at them just as they were about to bite her. The fire connected with their bodies—two birds with one stone. They cried in pain, landed on the ground, and tumbled away before disappearing underground. With a moment of safety, Morgan wheeled around to see if everybody was okay. She saw Emily hack one of the groundlings with her hatchet, and blood sprayed across her face. It landed on the ground with a thud, motionless. Emily kicked it away, looking totally grossed out. Arik had already knocked one creature down with her Bo staff and shoved her weapon into the mouth of another. She swung her staff over her head and tossed the groundling deep into the woods. It screamed as it disappeared into the black. Meanwhile, Mahihkan had a creature in either paw. One he was tearing apart with his teeth, while the other, limp and half chewed, had already suffered the same fate. His mouth was dripping with blood. He tossed the two creatures into the fire.

Another shriek came from behind Morgan. She'd been watching the other three fight groundlings, but now she swiveled around to defend herself. Emily was there already. She swung the hatchet and connected with the creature in midair. It fell to the ground in two pieces. She flipped the hatchet in the air and caught it by the handle, then made eye contact with Morgan.

"I *also* play tennis," she said, explaining the impeccable aim.

"Maybe I should take it up," Morgan said.

"Why? Are we going to make a habit out of fighting these things?"

"God, I hope not."

"Focus, you two," Mahihkan said.

Emily got back into place, and as more shrieking filled the air another barrage of groundlings came flying at them.

They were fought off like the first wave, and a small pile of the creatures began to form at the feet of the four travelers.

"At least they suck at fighting," Emily said.

"They're like zombies, though," Morgan said. "They don't know when to quit."

"There are too many of these beastly things," Arik said with disgust. "We can't keep this up forever."

"That's the spirit," Mahihkan grumbled, as he caught another groundling before it connected with the squirrel's shoulder. He didn't bother biting this one, opting to simply throw it into the fire. The groundling squealed and then shriveled into a tiny ball. Moments later, the wolf let out a howl. He reached down and pulled off one that had attached itself to his leg.

"They're coming out of the ground now!" Emily said.

"That means we can't hear them coming," Morgan said.

The groundlings began popping out of the earth at a furious pace, and the group directed their weapons to the ground, striking and kicking the creatures as they surfaced.

"This is like whack-a-mole times a thousand!" Emily said.

"Way less fun, though!" Morgan said, kicking another as it tried to bite her leg. "What are they trying to do?!"

"They're trying to suck our blood!" Mahihkan said.

"What? Like vampires?" Morgan asked.

"That's why there isn't much game around these parts! Any living thing, they cling to!" Mahihkan said.

"Freaking ground leeches!" Emily said.

"That's a way better name than groundlings!" Morgan said.

"How do we stop them?" Arik said.

The groundlings kept sticking their snouts into the air from under the dirt floor of the northern woods, biting at the human and animal beings. The creatures were either hit with a weapon or with a foot and disappeared underground, only to reappear and attack again.

Arik's question went unanswered until Emily said, "They're attracted to movement and warmth, right?"

"Yes!" The wolf was busy dealing with a large group that had come at him through the air. They were attacking in all ways now—through the air, from the ground—adapting to fight more effectively. They were apparently far more intelligent than any of the beings had given them credit for.

"What if we put out the fire?" Emily said.

Mahihkan and Arik looked at each other dumbfounded, undoubtedly questioning why they'd not thought of that earlier.

"Why haven't you brought this girl to the North Country before?" Arik asked Morgan.

"At least I brought her here now!" Morgan said.

"How about we stay alive so I can come again?" Emily said.

She dropped her hatchet to start throwing dirt onto the fire with both hands. Even when a groundling flew through the air and attached itself to her back, she screamed in pain but wouldn't stop. Morgan pressed her smoldering torch into the creature and it screeched, then let go.

"You guys put out the fire. I'll make sure they don't get you!" Morgan said.

Emily was joined by Arik and Mahihkan. The animal beings were excellent diggers, and when they got going, dirt showered over the fire in thick clouds of black. Meanwhile Morgan whacked the groundlings away before they could attach themselves to skin or hide. In seconds, the last of the flames had gasped for life, and as soon as the fire was out, the groundlings began to disperse, and then retreat altogether.

Exhausted, and only after Mahihkan had checked to make sure none of the creatures had attached themselves to Eli, the group collapsed, sitting around what had once been the fire. Morgan dropped the torch she'd been using and quickly snuffed it out.

"Nobody move for a bit so they can't feel where we are," Mahihkan said. "We should be alright. They'll go off looking for something else."

"What were they doing attaching themselves to the tree roots?" Emily asked.

"They'll feed off any living thing," Mahihkan said. "It's why," he pointed at the trees and their naked branches, "the trees are bare closer to the ground and the brush. It's why this place is . . . a dead place."

"Speaking of dead things . . ." Morgan found that the words weren't coming out all that easily. She felt exhausted. "What are . . . you . . ." She started to see spots blacker than the night that shrouded them now that the fire was doused. "What're you . . . doing . . . alive?"

"That's a long story, Morgan," Mahihkan said.

"I . . . I . . ."

But Morgan couldn't utter another word. It was as if all her energy, all her life, had left her body, as though Mistapew was with her now, sucking out *her* soul. The black spots almost filled her vision entirely, and she began to sway.

"Morgan!" Arik said.

"There's one stuck to her back!" Emily said.

Before Morgan lost consciousness, she saw Emily rush over to her, her arms out, ready to catch her before she collapsed.

EIGHT

Morgan was walking across the Barren Grounds, to the west, towards the mountain range that she'd crossed with Eli, Arik, and Ochek to discover the place where Mason had been holding the summer birds for many years, leaving so many villagers in Misewa to starve, sometimes to death, as a result.

She knew she was dreaming.

Hovering over the highest mountain, farther north than she'd been before, was a hole in the sky letting in brightness that shone down like a spotlight. Eight arms extended from the hole and spiraled around it protectively. The hole and the arms looked like a small-scale Milky Way. It was the most beautiful thing Morgan had ever seen, and she reached for it, as though she could touch it, as though she could gather in its light, hold it inside of her, and force out the pain she'd been doing her best to ignore.

In the blink of an eye, Morgan was on the mountain peak, showered by the light, staring up at the hole in the sky, still reaching, still wanting to pull all the light into her chest. She could tell then that there weren't arms extending from the hole. It was a spider, as big as a constellation, that had wrapped its legs around the hole in the sky.

Then an oval object, glowing white, appeared at the center of the hole, and lowered itself towards earth, towards Morgan, on a single strand of web. It continued its descent until it landed in her outstretched hands. Once safely within her grasp, the stone broke off from the web, which remained where it was, dangling there from the sky to the earth, dancing like billowing smoke.

Morgan held the stone to her chest, and, once pressed there, close to her heart, it turned red. At that exact moment, the light went out from within the hole in the sky, brightness to blackness, as though Creator himself had flicked off a switch. The spider's legs straightened and stretched to the horizon in eight directions. The legs gathered dark gray clouds all around the hole, and the hole then looked like the mouth of a cave, cold and black.

The hole began to grow. Darkness spread everywhere, swallowing everything into it. It drew ever closer to Morgan, and the closer it came, the brighter red the stone glowed. When the black had covered all of the North Country except the oval stone, lightning flashed high above, and appeared to take the shape of pictures that Morgan had seen countless times on the walls of the Council Hut. But the bolts of electricity were gone too fast to reveal what it was trying to say, what story it was trying to tell. The flashes of lightning were followed by a rumbling thunder, guttural roars that shook the earth underneath Morgan's feet. She could feel it through her moccasins.

They were coming again. The groundlings. The entire mountain was vibrating. Morgan fell to her knees, and buried the stone within her arms, firm against her chest.

"Morgan," a voice said.

"Eli?" she said. "Is that you?" It sounded like her brother, but she couldn't see him. "Where are you?"

"Morgan."

Her name was repeated by another voice. Emily's.

Morgan opened her eyes to find herself inside the tent, lying down face to face with her friend. She was sweating all over her body. She could feel that her top was damp. She could feel chilly sweat sliding off her forehead. She lifted her hand, which took a monumental effort, and wiped some sweat away, at least enough so that it stopped dripping into her eyes.

"What?" Morgan asked groggily.

"You were pretty much yelling," Emily said.

"I was dreaming," Morgan said.

"Dreaming? It sounded more like a nightmare to me."

"It . . ." It was already fading away from her. "It was a dream, and *then* it was a nightmare. There was a light, and then . . . darkness. There was a stone."

"Just a stone? Like . . . what kind of stone?" Emily asked.

"I don't know. It was . . . smooth and . . . glowing, like, different colors." Morgan tried to remember everything that had happened. It came to her in flashes, like the lightning. Walking on the Barren Grounds. The hole over the mountain that shone bright, then covered everything in black, like spilled ink. The spider wrapping its legs around the hole as though keeping it close, or trying to control it. The oval stone, glowing . . . white. Yes. White, then red. The thunder bellowing like a wild beast. Somebody calling her name. "I can't explain it."

"Are you okay?" Emily asked. She put her hand on Morgan's forehead, checking her temperature.

"I'm fine," Morgan said, softly lifting Emily's hand away.

"Who knows how much blood that thing sucked from your body," Emily reasoned. "It could be why—"

"The dream meant something," Morgan said, rubbing her head, which hurt almost as much as when she'd been struck by Muskwa in the southern woods. "It had to have. It wasn't some, like, hallucination from blood loss. I think . . . I think Eli was there with me. I swear I heard him."

"Maybe he was," Emily said. "He's been on your mind a lot. When you think about something, or somebody, a lot, you dream of whatever you've been thinking about. It could've just been that. That doesn't make it a hallucination."

"That's true, I guess," Morgan admitted. "I guess it just felt like . . . more."

"Well, you'll figure it out," Emily said. Then she shrugged. "We've got lots of walking ahead of us, right?"

Morgan nodded.

"So you've got lots of time to think."

"Yeah." But even then, the dream, the nightmare, whatever it was, continued to slip away, as if it were being enveloped in the black as everything else had been. The only thing that remained clear was the stone, cradled in her arms, breathing calm into her chest. "That stone. It was like a piece of the moon that fell to earth." Morgan rubbed her face, shut her eyes hard, then opened them, trying to wake herself up.

"A moon stone," Emily stated.

"Exactly," Morgan said.

It was still dark out, still night, but light enough as Morgan's eyes adjusted that she could see around the inside of the tent. There was Emily, looking at her with concern. There was Eli, covered by a hide blanket, his eyes closed and unmoving. Had he called to her from where he was? Was that even possible? She'd heard him, but hadn't seen him. Maybe Emily was right. Maybe it was just that he'd been on her mind. But then, her mother had been on her mind as well, and Morgan hadn't dreamed of her.

Arik was on the other side of Morgan, sound asleep, curled up into a furry little ball, as if nothing at all had happened. As if they hadn't been in a life-or-death fight with sharp-toothed, red-eyed creatures that sucked blood out of your body with their weird tongues. As if Morgan hadn't, according to Emily, screamed herself awake. Arik was snoring, and probably dreaming a happy dream. Not a dream that was as terrifying as it was mystifying.

"Mahihkan?" Morgan asked. "Is he . . ."

"Keeping watch," Emily said. "He's super intense, hey?"

"Ya think? I thought Ochek was intense, but Mahihkan is next-level."

"I think it's his eyes," Emily said. "They're like headlights. Like, high beams."

"Has he been out there all night?" Morgan asked.

Emily nodded. "He refused to let anybody else stay up. He said that nothing would hurt the boy while he was around."

"He was the wolf that saved us, when Mason was going to shoot us with a bow and arrow. He could have been safe with Mason, but he protected us instead," Morgan explained. "And he did it because of Eli, I think. They had this weird bond that I've never been able to understand, but to Eli . . . losing Mahihkan was almost as bad as losing Ochek."

"*That* wolf was the one that saved you guys?" Emily said. "I thought he died."

"I thought he died, too." Morgan pictured Mahihkan tackling Mason, and both of them rolling over the edge of the cliff. She saw the wolf hanging on for dear life, dangling over the river below. She saw him falling, those yellow eyes disappearing into the swift water. "I guess I was wrong."

"That's crazy, to survive a fall like that," Emily said. "Back from the dead. Hopefully we can do the same with Eli."

"Eli is *not* dead."

"I'm sorry," Emily said quickly. "I meant . . ."

"No," Morgan said, "you don't have to be sorry. I just need him to be okay. He can't die."

"He won't die. We'll save him."

"There's not many people in the world, our world, that I have left to lose, and I can't lose them. Eli, the grandma I've never met, Katie and James." Morgan glanced at Emily.

"And somebody who'd drop everything and come to my house super early in the morning without asking why."

"Oh yeah? Who's that?" Emily chuckled.

"Gee, I wonder."

"Sounds like another mystery."

They stared at each other through the dark for a few minutes, in a comfortable silence, and then Morgan asked, "So, how's your trip to Askí so far?"

"Oh, you know, everything's exciting with you around. Art class, killer ground leeches . . ."

"Those were totally fun." Morgan reached around and felt where the creature had bit her. There were dressings over the wound, and it was sore to the touch. "Are *you* okay? I know one of them—"

"I'm okay," Emily assured her. "You saved me, remember?"

"And you saved me."

"I didn't save you so much as I caught you."

"I keep worrying . . ." Morgan trailed off and shook her head.

"You keep worrying . . ." Emily prompted. "What?"

"Never mind," Morgan said. "It's stupid."

"What did I tell you at school the other day, Morg? The day we defeated the bullies."

"I don't know."

"You do *so* know," Emily said. "I told you not to lie to me, and you said you wouldn't."

"I vaguely remember that."

"Okay, so, what do you keep worrying?"

"I keep worrying that one day you're going to realize that you never should have been friends with me, and you'll stop talking to me, and you won't be dead but I'll still lose you."

"Morgan," Emily said, "that's not going to happen."

"But I seem distant all the time and I worry that you think I'm distant and I'm totally not. I blow up at people, I cry a lot, I travel to another world every night, I . . ." Morgan sat up and buried her face in her hands. "Who wants a friend like that? Look." She lifted her face and showed Emily her wet cheeks. Tears were sliding down her face. "See? I'm crying again."

"I don't care about any of that." Emily sat up, too, and she slid over to sit right beside Morgan. "What do you want to be? Boring? That's a *B* word that I'm not, and you're not either. I like that you're not afraid to cry in front of me. I think it's cool that you travel to another world every night."

"You do?"

Emily reached over and wiped a tear away from Morgan's cheek. "The whole not lying thing counts for me, too. So yes, I do, and stop it. Now I know you're delirious."

"You're awesome," Morgan said.

"I know." Emily put her arm around Morgan and coaxed her to lie back down with a gentle tug on her shoulder. Morgan obliged, and soon they were lying beside each other, staring up at the opening at the top of the tent, where the sky was visible through the trees. It was a dark shade of cyan blue. Dawn was breaking.

"Get some rest, okay?" Emily said.

But Morgan, who'd turned on her side and thrown her arm around Emily, was already fast asleep.

NINE

In the morning, the group built a modest fire on top of a platform that they'd constructed out of rocks. The size of the fire and its foundation were designed to not attract the groundlings. And as they started to eat breakfast without interruption, it became apparent that the creatures either didn't feel the warmth of the flames or simply wanted nothing more to do with the group. A large number of them had been killed the night before, and they were probably smart enough to want to live. Whatever the reason, it made the morning less stressful, as stew and tea were devoured.

They reviewed last night's battle, each one taking a turn to talk about the groundlings they'd fought. This prompted Arik to check Morgan's wound for the hundredth time that morning and apply more medicines so that it wouldn't become infected. Morgan revealed to Mahihkan that she'd noticed him following them, which the wolf didn't believe. He thought he'd been stealthy, but Emily insisted that

Morgan was telling the truth, that she'd seen yellow eyes deep in the forest.

"If you want to be really stealthy you should get sunglasses," Emily said. "Otherwise, you did great."

"Sunglasses?" Mahihkan said.

Emily explained what sunglasses were, and it was funny for Morgan to watch her friend try to describe something from earth to an animal being in Askí, something Morgan herself had done countless times before. Thanks to Eli and Morgan, Misewa's inhabitants knew all about driver's licenses, iPads, cartoons, attics, middle school, the internet ("You can ask this . . . internet . . . things you need to know and it speaks to you? Is it Creator you speak to?" "No, it's Google"), coffee, and so on.

Finally, Morgan had wondered about something long enough, and couldn't go any longer without knowing. Surely Arik wanted to know, too, and even Emily, who'd heard about Eli and Morgan's first journey to the North Country in detail now.

Morgan waited until sunglasses had been explained ("They protect your eyes from the sunlight, and plus they look cool") and then she asked Mahihkan, "How are you alive right now?"

Mahihkan finished chewing a spoonful of stew and sat quietly for a moment. It looked as if he had gone there, had traveled back in time just as Morgan and Eli had.

"The last thing I remember," he said, "is hitting the water."

Mahihkan went on to tell his story. After hitting the water, he was knocked unconscious, and he wasn't sure how long he was out cold. He wasn't sure how far the river carried him before he woke up and washed ashore in an unfamiliar forest. He'd ended up somewhere east, at the end of the world. It was why Mahihkan named the forest World's End.

"Another pretty obvious name, but still cool," Emily whispered to Morgan, who nodded her agreement.

Mahihkan found Mason farther down the shore, and he had not been so lucky. He was cold and long dead, probably having died after hitting the water from such a great height. The wolf left Mason as carrion for the ravens, and pulled himself away from the river and into the forest. He was tired and broken. He crawled through World's End for a long while, eating anything that he wasn't too weak to catch. It helped him survive those first days. But soon the pain from the broken bones in his body became too great, and at some point he passed out. He woke up in a village hidden deep within World's End, occupied by animal beings he had never met or seen before.

The village was called Ministik, or Island, because it had been built in a large clearing in the middle of a thick sea of green forest. The villagers were at once similar to and distinct from the beings of Misewa. They, too, were bipedal. They lived in dwellings with three walls insulated by caribou skins and a fourth wall made of tree trunks, the cracks filled with moss. These were perhaps cruder than the longhouses in Misewa, but just as warm and habitable. Their dress was comparable as well, but the villagers of Ministik painted their faces and bodies with red ocher.

Weeks after being brought into the village, and having been nursed back to health, Mahihkan left.

He traveled farther east until he came to a vast body of water, as big and as blue as the sky. From there, he went north and started on his way back to the North Country. Eventually, he came to the northern woods, and this was two years after waking up by the river on the shores of World's End (which, as it turned out, was not the end of the world at all). Since that time, Mahihkan had lived in the forest. Occasionally, he'd seen the children arrive through the Great Tree, and kept watch over them as they crossed the Barren Grounds. And then, yesterday, he'd seen the three of them walking in the northern woods, seen Eli being dragged on the sled, and decided to follow them. To protect them if needed.

"And you needed protection, after all," Mahihkan said as he finished his story.

"So you've been living in the northern woods for, like, four years?" Morgan asked.

"I guess I have," Mahihkan said.

"How are you not dead?"

The wolf scraped the rest of his food into his mouth, chewed, then responded. "As it turns out, I'm hard to kill."

"Are you going to come with us?" Emily asked. "I mean, actually with us?"

"I didn't save the boy's life," he put his hand on Eli's chest, right over his heart, "only so he can die like this. Yes, I'll come with you."

"Almost sounds like there weren't two other people saved along with Eli, hey?" Morgan said to Arik and Emily.

"Yes, I seem to remember that we, too, were rescued along with your brother," Arik said to Morgan.

"If not for the boy," Mahihkan spoke in a growl, "you would be dead, and don't forget it for one second."

"*There's* the Mahihkan I know and love," Morgan said.

"Whatever the case, I'm glad you'll be walking with us." Arik flung her pack over her back. "You may be good at living, but you suck at hiding."

The camp was taken down, packs were shouldered, and weapons were grasped, just in case the groundlings decided to show their ugly faces again. The group traveled ever deeper into the northern woods, walking as softly as they could so as not to alert the creatures to their presence. The forest seemed endless, and Arik, Emily, and Morgan were glad that Mahihkan insisted on pulling Eli's sled, trusting nobody else to keep the boy alive. Yesterday's journey had been difficult to begin with, but pulling the sled had made it much harder. The wolf seemed tireless, leading the other three onward. He, of course, had walked the same path in his years spent in the northern woods, and had even seen Mistapew, albeit rarely. But he'd never dared follow the trail to its end, had never had a reason to until now.

Arik and Emily talked nonstop those first hours, while Morgan kept to herself. She couldn't stop thinking about her dream. She'd managed to remember a great deal of it by replaying it over and over, but she still couldn't decipher what it meant.

"Dreams are powerful," Arik had said. "Dreams help us make sense of the world in ways that we can't while we're awake."

Maybe they did, Morgan thought, but something more on the nose would've been helpful. Like if she'd dreamed of the kind of map you saw in pirate movies: there'd be a big *X* to mark where Eli's soul was. As it stood, she was left with a hole in the sky, a glowing stone attached to a web, gray clouds, gathering darkness, lightning bolts, and rolling thunder.

In what world did any of that make sense?

TEN

The day wore on. The sun climbed higher, though it was mostly blotted out by the thick canopy of leaves far above. The path continued, stubbornly refusing to lead the travelers to its completion. They hadn't yet stopped, not even for lunch. Morgan was tired and hungry, and she could tell that Emily and Arik were, too. But Mahihkan forged ahead, pulling Eli with him, and the sight of his determination was enough to motivate the others to keep going. Morgan knew that on this, the second day of their journey, her brother's time was getting shorter with each passing moment.

"He must be so thirsty," Morgan said to Emily, as the trees began to thin out and they could see the sun clearly for the first time in two days.

They were entering a clearing, something they hadn't seen yet, and the temperature shifted from cold to warm as soon as they stepped into the brightness. For the next couple of minutes, as they crossed the open ground, it felt as though they weren't in such a dreary place. But even still, a dreary feeling persisted. Eli's body would be starting to break down. He'd not had water in well over a day, and they had only two days left to save his life. Every once in a while Arik was dabbing a wet cloth against his lips, but that was doing very little for him.

"I'm not sure whether he even knows he's thirsty," Emily said. "I know that's crappy, but he's probably not suffering. His body is, but he's somewhere else. Right?"

Morgan shook her head, glanced at the sun, then ahead at her brother. He was losing color, his face was sunken, his hair was drying out.

"Just over two weeks ago, I didn't think anybody had a soul. I would've thought he was in a coma or something. Out of everything I've seen over here, including just being here at all, that's what feels most surreal to me." Morgan stuck both hands out in front of her and held them as though she were cupping water. "I literally saw Creator's hands. They were, like, right in front of me."

"I know," Emily said. "That part of your story's pretty memorable." She proceeded to recap what Morgan had told her. "Ochek floating in midair after falling from the sequoia, the ball of light forming underneath his body, tendrils growing from the ball and turning into fricking *fingers*. The big, ethereal hands lifting Ochek into space, and him becoming a constellation. No big deal, he just turned into stars."

Her tone was nonchalant, but her eyes were awestruck.

"Ochekatchakosuk," Morgan said.

"That's so wild."

Morgan lifted one hand in the air, like it was Creator's hand bringing Ochek closer and closer to the sky. "If there's a Creator, then we have souls, and if we have souls, you're right. At least he's not suffering. Just us. We're suffering."

Morgan stopped walking, and so did Emily. They were in the middle of the clearing. She raised both arms up and stretched her hands towards the heavens, right where, if it were night, Ochek's constellation would be. That was where *his* soul was, Morgan was sure of it. Then another thought struck her, and she let her arms fall, her hands slapping against her thighs. She started to cry, and because Emily had no idea why Morgan was crying, she went and wrapped her arms tightly around her. Morgan, in turn, threw her arms around Emily and buried her face into Emily's shoulder.

"I know it doesn't make this any better," Emily said.

"The thing is," Morgan said, "I know he has a soul, and I know it's somewhere, but if his body dies and we don't find where his soul is, it'll be trapped like Kihiw's. Eli won't go to heaven or the stars or wherever souls are supposed to go. He'll be stuck wherever he is forever."

"We'll find it. I promise."

"And I'll be stuck, too. I'll never be the same. Not without him. Why can't I figure out what the stupid dream was trying to tell me?"

"I don't know." Emily started to shush Morgan, who was sobbing uncontrollably. "Shhhh. It'll be okay. Shhhh. It's okay. Shhhh. It's okay."

They stood there, holding each other, Morgan crying into Emily's sweater and Emily shushing her friend. After a minute or so, Morgan began to relax. She took deep breaths in through her nose, and let them out slowly through her mouth. She did this again and again, and eventually turned her head so that her cheek was pressed against Emily's shoulder. She could see Mahihkan and Arik waiting patiently at the edge of the clearing.

"I told you all I do is cry," Morgan whispered.

"And I told you that's one thing out of millions of things I like about you," Emily whispered back.

"You're crazy, you know that?"

"I've been told that once or twice," Emily said.

"Let's just do this for another minute," Morgan said, "and pretend that we're somewhere safe and Eli's okay."

"I think we can spare another minute."

And so they stayed in one another's embrace for an extra minute.

During that time, for the most part, Morgan was able to stay calm, because everything felt calm. The air was warm, there was no breeze, the sun was shining down on them. It was easy, in fact, to pretend that they were somewhere safe, because it felt as though they were. It seemed as though this was the one place in the northern woods that offered safe harbor. Morgan closed her eyes, shut herself off from the world, and almost, just almost, found herself able to pretend Eli was okay. She tried only to feel what was right in front of her. Her arms wrapped around Emily's neck, Emily's arms snug around her waist, her tears soaked into the fabric of Emily's sweater, but she also felt something else, a sensation that her legs were trembling.

Morgan lifted her head.

"You ready?" Emily asked.

"No, it's . . ."

Morgan focused on the feeling in her legs. She went through a list in her mind of what it could be. Was she over-tired? Maybe. Was she anxious? Definitely. Had they been walking too long without stopping? Was it from the blood loss she'd suffered the night before? All these things were possible. It could have been all of them combined.

"I think it's nothing," Morgan said. "Maybe we should rest soon. I need to rest for a little while."

"See if you can convince Mahihkan of that," Emily said.

"Or you could carry me."

"Lie in the sled beside Eli," Emily said. "The wolf won't even notice."

"Look at you, solving problems."

"That's what I do."

They let go of each other, and Morgan took one step towards their waiting companions, who, by now, weren't waiting all that patiently. Mahihkan paced back and forth next to the sled while Arik had perched on it, tapping the wood with her heels restlessly. Morgan took only one step, then stopped, and froze.

"What is it?" Emily asked.

"Shhh," Morgan said sharply.

Emily, who was about to follow Morgan, stopped in her tracks, and they both stood in place. Morgan focused on the shakiness of her legs, and the more she focused the more she realized that it was not that she was tired, it was not that she'd lost blood, it was not that they'd walked a long while without stopping, and it was not anxiety. She could feel the ground vibrating under the soles of her moccasins, just like last night. She looked up from her feet to the ground in front of them. The long, dry grass in the clearing appeared still, as though she were staring at a photograph. The whole world seemed unmoving, until one single blade of grass flickered like a flame dancing from a distant breath. This movement set off a chain reaction, as though it woke up the entire field, and in no time the grass was moving in rolling waves.

"Oh no," Emily said.

"They're back," Morgan said.

"Morgan! Emily! Run!" Arik cried from the other side of the clearing, jumping off the sled.

She was maybe thirty yards away, but it may as well have been a mile. Morgan could see the groundlings through the grass, burrowing through the dirt, their backs bulging out of the earth, leaving behind protruding trails.

"We can't move," Morgan whispered to Emily. "I don't think they know we're here right now."

"Then what are they doing?" Emily asked.

"I don't know. Maybe it's because the clearing is so much warmer than the woods."

"That doesn't explain why they aren't coming near us."

Emily was right. There were more and more ground-lings with each passing second, so many that the trails they left behind made the clearing look like one big trench garden. The dried grass was almost all uprooted. This was happening everywhere except right where Emily and Morgan stood—the groundlings knew where they were but refused to attack. Whatever the reason was, it was a relief, because there were hundreds of them, and there was no way the pair would be able to fight them off. Even if Mahihkan and Arik were with them, it would be a slaughter. But what were they to do? Stand there all day until the sun died, until the warmth left, until the dark and the cool air pulled the groundlings away to somewhere else?

"They're circling us like sharks," Morgan said. "Why do sharks circle people? Do they actually do that or is that just in movies?"

"No, I think they actually do that," Emily said, "and it's not good."

"Maybe we should just run for it."

"I don't see what else we can do. At some point they're going to come flying out of the ground and suck the life out of us."

Morgan shivered at the thought of another groundling attaching itself to her body and drinking her blood.

"You have to move!" Mahihkan called out. "Now!"

"Whoever thought that the biggest danger in the northern woods wouldn't be Mistapew but a bunch of Christmas logs with sharp teeth," Morgan said.

"And super creepy red eyes," Emily added.

"And the shrieking and the tongues."

Emily reached into her backpack and pulled out the hatchet. Morgan thought about getting her slingshot out, but once again she couldn't see the use of it. She wished that she'd chosen a different weapon. Like a flamethrower.

"I'll go first," Emily said, gripping the hatchet firmly.

"I'll be right behind you," Morgan said.

"Ready?" Emily had taken a track and field stance, set to run.

Morgan nodded. It was now or never. "Ready."

"On three," Emily said. "One. Two. Th—"

As they were about to take off over the miniature trenches, all at once the creatures stopped circling the girls and disappeared underground. As quickly as they had come, they were gone. The only difference was that the clearing now looked as if it had been broken up by a garden tiller. It was silent, but it wasn't calm. There was no peace to the stillness.

"This can't be good," Morgan said.

"I think we should still run," Emily said.

"That's probably wise."

The girls sprinted from the middle of the clearing towards Mahihkan, Arik, and Eli, but they hadn't gone more than a few yards when they heard a cracking noise behind them. It stopped them cold.

"Keep coming!" Arik shouted.

"Don't look back!" Mahihkan yelled.

Of course, when somebody tells you not to look, the first thing you're going to do is look. Morgan spun around to see what was making the cracking sound. Across the clearing, not that far off in the woods, trees were falling over, and whatever was doing it was closing in. Even more trees were bursting from the earth, right from their roots. The ground was shaking fiercely. Then something huge beneath the earth began to surface at the edge of the clearing. It was making the same sort of trail the groundlings made, only six feet higher.

"Oh crap," Emily whispered.

"Run!" Morgan screamed.

The girls turned and ran. Morgan could feel the ground shake more and more aggressively. It was gaining on them. They were twenty yards away from the others. Fifteen. Mahihkan picked Eli up from the sled and ran into the forest. Arik stood in place, her arms out towards the girls as if she was going to catch them. Her eyes weren't on Emily and Morgan, though. They were high above them, and wide with terror.

"Keep running!" she said.

A deafening shriek filled the clearing, filled all the northern woods, and then the ground stopped shaking. Morgan and Emily ran even faster. Ten yards. Five. Arik turned and ran into the woods when the girls hit the tree line. By then, Morgan knew what was happening. All those groundlings had cleared the way for one massive creature that was now flying through the air towards them.

Inside the forest they kept running and didn't slow down. The trees overhead cracked as the giant groundling dove towards the earth. Morgan saw that Arik and Mahihkan had ducked into a large animal's den in a raised area off to the side.

"Here!" Mahihkan shouted.

"Quickly!" Arik said.

Morgan took Emily's hand and guided her towards it. Trees to either side started to fall. It was almost on top of them. When the snapping was right over their heads, they leapt for the den as the monster slammed into the earth.

ELEVEN

As soon as Morgan and Emily had dived into the den, Morgan turned onto her back to see what had been chasing them and caught a glimpse of the monster before it tunneled underground. It was like a zoomed-in view of the groundlings. The same eyes, teeth, and tongue. Its skin was like a caterpillar's, segmented and covered in tiny legs, with larger legs at the front that it used to jump out of the dirt. It was entirely black except for translucent squares along its body that showed stores of blood. The monster shrieked one last time, out of frustration, Morgan guessed, before diving below the earth's surface. When the tremors stopped and the group was sure the thing was gone, they crawled out of the den and stood around a massive crater the giant groundling had left behind.

Emily slumped forward but stopped herself from falling by bracing her hands against her knees. "We're all going to die trying to save Eli, aren't we?"

"Do you want to turn back?" Morgan asked.

Emily took a deep breath and straightened up, then brushed off the suggestion as if it were foolish. "No, of course not, I'm just saying . . ." She motioned to the crater with both arms, indicating its girth as though the other three couldn't already see it. "Do these things keep getting bigger and bigger? Like in Star Wars with all the Death Stars?"

"I can't imagine a groundling bigger than that one," Arik remarked. "In fact, in this case, 'groundling' is probably not the best name."

"That was the mother," Mahihkan said, still holding Eli. "And you're right, Arik. I doubt you'll find a bigger one in these woods."

"Hopefully a bigger one won't find *us*," Emily said. "If we survive this and I come back again, we're *not* going groundling hunting." She looked at Morgan. "*Ever.*"

"I was just going to say that I'm okay with hunting prairie chickens," Morgan said. "What about the father, if that was the mother? Are you sure there isn't—"

"The mother kills the father after their babies are born," Mahihkan said. "It helps to give the babies sustenance."

"Romantic," Emily said.

"Personally, I'm surprised those mean little things are only babies," Arik said.

"They're doing what's in their nature," Mahihkan said.

"Like you were, when you tried to kill me and Eli and Ochek and Arik?" Morgan asked.

"Yes," Mahihkan said matter-of-factly, "and if you weren't who you are, I'd have killed you all by now and not thought twice about it."

"That's comforting," Emily grumbled.

"It doesn't have to be," Mahihkan said. "Look, we can spend all day arguing about why the creatures on Askí do what they do, or we can save this boy's life."

There was no discussion after that. The group had a quick meal, not wasting time to heat anything up, then got their packs. The sled, which Mahihkan had left behind in the clearing, was destroyed, so the wolf draped Eli over his shoulders. They walked at a quicker pace, albeit lightly, through the northern woods, deciding that from here on out they would avoid not only fires, but sunlight and warmth altogether. It would make the journey dark, but safe. Or, as safe as it could be.

The path led down an embankment, and they carefully descended to where the ground flattened out. At the bottom, there was a stream of crystal clear, cool water. They afforded themselves a moment to fill up their canteens, wash their faces, and drink right from the stream. On either side of the water, the grass was lush and vibrantly green, which they hadn't seen yet in the woods. Even the grass in the clearing, full of the sun and its warmth, had been dried out. That feeling of life kept them there for longer than they'd planned to stay, but even Mahihkan didn't complain. And Eli got to taste some of it, too, as Arik dabbed his lips with a dampened cloth; this was the only time that gesture didn't seem futile to Morgan.

With their bodies refreshed from the life-giving water,

they continued with renewed fortitude. The path wound through dead trees, curving to the west for a long while, then turning back east, rarely leading them straight. But they kept to it, rather than cutting through the underbrush and risking an encounter with any other strange creatures. The groundlings had been enough to handle.

Eventually, the path flattened out, and at that point the group saw something they'd been dreaming about since embarking on the journey deep into the woods to save Eli: the end of the line. The route continued straight until it ran into a cliff face, obscured by massive trees. Their excitement was quickly tempered by the awareness that this only meant the path was at its end—their quest might still have to continue, and with nothing left to guide them. As well, they had, perhaps, a small mountain to climb over or walk around.

As they came to the path's end, however, Morgan knew that they wouldn't need to go any farther. She could see a large, round opening in the cliff's rocky, gray surface.

"Look. That's got to be the mouth of a cave."

She was the first to step right up and look inside. What she saw were drawings. The walls of the cave were covered in them. She inspected them carefully, running her hands over each one, and saw that they weren't all that different from the illustrations on the Council Hut walls. They were painted with red ocher, and when she followed them, she found that they, too, told stories, from one picture to the next. One in particular caught her eye. It showed animal beings, hunters, gathered on one side of a thick and tall tree that looked to be on fire. Curvy lines rose from it to indicate flames. Rising high above the tree and the flames was an eagle, its wings outstretched, its face pointing towards the heavens.

"This is Kihiw," Morgan said. "This is his story."

"So it is," Arik said. "Although, I don't recognize this part of it."

Morgan kept looking at it, memorizing every line that had been drawn. "It's like, this is the *end* of the story. It hasn't happened yet." She watched the eagle as though it might actually fly away. "Why is it so familiar, then?" she asked herself.

Mahihkan didn't consider the drawing all that important. He had carefully lowered Eli to the ground beside the path and now was looking at all of them, one then another, an annoyed expression on his already surly face.

"We need to worry less about an eagle that's been dead for ages, and more about this boy who's dying *right now*. Look for a clue, look for anything at all, just don't look at those stupid drawings."

"Yeah. Yeah, you're right," Morgan said, unconvincingly.

She turned away and began to search in earnest along with the others. They looked everywhere. All along either side of the cliff face, on the ground where the path ended, but nothing looked like a place where a soul might be kept. What were they even searching for? Something that would fit well in a fantasy story? A locked, golden chest? An urn of some kind, or a bottle with a stopper you had to take out to release a trapped soul?

Morgan couldn't get the ocher drawings out of her mind and kept glancing back at the cave's entrance. They seemed familiar somehow, and more than that, the cave itself seemed familiar. The round opening. The darkness within it.

"If it's not out here, Eli's soul has to be in Mistapew's dwelling," Mahihkan said, after minutes of fruitlessly searching everywhere outside the mouth of the cave. "The giant would want it close."

"So you want us to . . ." Arik pointed into the darkness, ". . . go into Mistapew's house and fumble around, looking for something Eli's soul could be in?"

"He may not be home," Mahihkan reasoned.

"Oh yeah," Emily said, "the giant could've just gone to the 7-Eleven to grab a Slurpee."

"He doesn't stay in his cave all day."

"What if he does?" Arik said. "What if he does until night, and only comes out then? Have you ever seen him in the daylight?"

Mahihkan thought a moment, then shook his head. "Not that I remember."

"That story with the eagle happened at night, and Eli's soul was taken at night," Emily said, "so maybe he *is* nocturnal."

"Which means he'll be in there right now," Arik whispered.

Through this entire exchange, Morgan had been backing away slowly from the cave, without ever taking her eyes off it, barely hearing what the others were saying. She backed away until she had a clear picture of everything all at once. The dark inside the cave. The entrance to it. The drawings that decorated the cliff face surrounding the opening. She closed her eyes and pictured her dream. She opened her eyes. She closed her eyes and saw the hole in the sky over the mountain. She opened her eyes and looked at the round entrance to the cave. She closed her eyes and saw the flashes of lightning in that odd pattern. She opened her eyes and saw the drawings, the intricate lines within each image mimicking the path of each lightning bolt. She closed her eyes and saw the moon stone being lowered into her hands. She opened her eyes, and they trailed away from the cave, towards an object near where she was standing, covered with dirt from the path. An inch of it, and no more, was exposed. Though easy to miss—they'd all walked by it—it was pure white. So white that in the relative darkness of the northern woods it appeared to be emitting light.

Morgan crouched over it and brushed dirt away with both hands, revealing the shape of the object, and what it was: an oval stone that had to have been placed there intentionally. An oval stone exactly like the one she'd dreamed of. Something, or somebody, had dug a hole, placed the rock inside it, and covered it with dirt from the path. One of the four of them must have inadvertently kicked dirt away while walking past it, and there it was.

"How is this possible?" she asked aloud, to nobody in particular.

"How is what possible?" Emily asked, and she was soon crouching beside Morgan.

"It *was* Eli, Emily. In my dreams. He called to me. It was really him. He came all the way there"—she picked up the stone and held it out in front of her—"from here." Morgan marveled at the stone's beauty, glowing white and perfectly smooth.

"He's . . . in *there*?" Emily asked.

By now, the other two had crouched down with Emily and Morgan. All of them were staring at the rock, and by the looks in their eyes, they all knew it to be true. It was now the most precious stone in all of Askí.

"He's in here," Morgan said, "there's no other explanation. Eli came to show me where he was, and to show me . . ." The last part of the dream came crashing into her mind. The ear-shattering thunder that had followed the lightning bolts.

"To show you what?" Emily asked.

A shiver ran up Morgan's spine. "The danger."

Morgan turned around slowly until she was facing the cave's entrance, and the others turned with her. At the exact second she finished turning, at the exact moment her gaze sank into the blackness, a piercing roar, like thunder, came from deep within it.

Everybody sprang up. Morgan cradled the stone in her arms, and pressed it so firmly against her chest that she could feel her heart beat against it. Mahihkan lifted Eli off the ground and wrapped the boy around his shoulders. They backed away as another roar came; this time it was closer.

"I think we woke him up," Arik said.

"I think we'd better start moving," Mahihkan said.

One final, cataclysmic roar exploded from the dark, and then Mistapew emerged from the cave. For a second, he just stood there. A hairy, humanoid creature, with eyes that eerily sparked with intelligence. And he was awfully big. Bigger than she'd imagined. He was at least ten feet tall.

His eyes dropped to look at the four travelers, standing yards away from the entrance to his den. He looked at each one of their faces, from left to right, until his eyes fixed on the moon stone. At the sight of the stone, he charged at them like a bullet fired from a gun.

"Run!" Morgan screamed, but she feared it was already too late.

TWELVE

They ran.

Despite Morgan's fears, despite how tired she was from all the walking, from only narrowly evading the mother groundling, she found the energy to run as fast as she ever had before. She was even keeping up with Emily, who was beside Mahihkan, Eli over his shoulders, hardly slowed by the extra weight. Arik, on all fours, was well ahead of everybody.

Mistapew's heavy footsteps sounded like a freight train coming up behind them.

The group followed the path back in the direction they'd come from. The giant gained on them on the straight section, coming so close to Morgan that once she felt his fingertips swipe across the back of her head. She held the moon stone closer and tighter, like a running back protecting a football, and leapt over the stream when they came to it with an agility she didn't think she had. Emily was at the top of the embankment by then, and took Morgan by the hand. She pulled her up and they kept going, not breaking stride to look back when they heard Mistapew slip on the embankment behind them. Morgan thought he must have gotten his feet wet in the stream.

"Split up and meet at the den!" Mahihkan called to the girls. "It's our only chance to lose him!"

The four branched off just as the path began to curve. Mahihkan barreled through the underbrush, not bothering to stay on the route at all. Arik darted off to the west, disappearing into the forest. Morgan dashed towards the den not far off from the trail, mindful not to lose her way, dodging trees and jumping over bushes and trying not to let the obstacles slow her down. She could hear Emily behind her. She knew it was her friend, as the footsteps were too light, too quick to be Mistapew's. She knew, as well, that Emily was keeping Morgan's pace, putting her friend's safety ahead of her own, as if, no matter what, their fates would be tied together.

By now, the giant had recovered. Morgan glanced back every few seconds and saw him closing the gap his stumble had created.

"We're not going to make it!" Morgan said to Emily. "He's too close!"

"Yes we are!" Emily said, and then she stopped.

Morgan turned all the way around and continued to move towards the den, running backwards, while asking, "What are you doing? He'll kill you!"

"Just keep going, Morgan! Trust me!"

"Emily, no!"

"Go! Now!"

Morgan wavered for a second more, long enough to watch Emily reach into her backpack while Mistapew bore down on her. Then she turned back around while still in motion. But she hadn't been watching what was ahead of her. She fell right into a bush and landed on her back, which knocked the wind out of her. She was now looking up at Emily, who had taken the hatchet out. Her arm was cocked behind her head, ready to throw it. Mistapew was about to lunge at her. She threw the hatchet and it whipped through the air, end over end, right towards the giant's head. He raised his forearm to block the weapon. It tore through his flesh and stuck into his arm with a thump. There was a shrill cry before the giant dropped to his knees in pain, trying to dislodge the weapon. Emily helped Morgan up, and they took the opportunity to race for the den before Mistapew could continue his dogged pursuit.

The clearing was ahead, the den was to their right, and Morgan could see Mahihkan and Arik silently, frantically motioning them over. They turned sharply off the path without looking where Mistapew was and ducked into the den. When they were safely inside, Mahihkan and Arik placed spruce boughs over the entrance, and they waited as the giant's footsteps drew closer and closer still. Arik held one finger over her mouth, as if Morgan and Emily needed to be told.

It wasn't long before Mistapew stopped on the path a few yards away from where they were hidden. Morgan could catch glimpses of him through the spruce boughs as he moved back and forth in front of the opening. He inspected the area, and then stopped and looked directly at their hiding spot. Morgan could scarcely breathe. She tucked the stone underneath her top to conceal its glow. The four of them, peering intently through the camouflaged entrance, were frozen in place as Mistapew continued to stare, seemingly right at them. Unbearable seconds passed, seconds that felt like hours, until, at long last, he looked away, arched his back, lifted his head towards the sky, and cried out. Then he continued on his way, searching for them.

"He might keep looking for us all night," Mahihkan warned. "This is his hunting time."

"And now we're what he's hunting," Morgan said, taking the stone out.

"So we'll stay here until morning," Arik said. "Clearly."

"And then what? How do we get Eli out of this thing?" Emily put her hand on the stone and started to rub it vigorously.

"It's not a lamp and Eli's not a genie, Em," Morgan said, managing a little smile.

"Well, you never know."

"We'll do everything we can to figure it out. Now that we have it, now that we have *him*, we can't fail, or else . . ." Morgan went from smiling to suppressing tears. She couldn't bear to finish the sentence. She couldn't bear to think of what she'd do if she lost him and her mother within days of each other. She cleared her throat.

"We've come too far to fail now."

"What if we just broke it open like an egg?" Arik suggested. "That's it! His soul might come oozing out and we could just stuff it into his mouth."

"That feels like a last resort kind of thing," Morgan said.

"Also a pretty disgusting thought," Emily added. "Can you imagine a soul being like an egg yolk?"

"Get some rest," Mahihkan said. "It's been a long day, and we have a lot to do come morning."

There was a lot to do, Morgan thought, and almost no time left in which to do it, because by tomorrow, they'd have only one day left.

Eli would have only one day left.

While the wolf had ordered the others to sleep, Morgan could tell he had no intention of doing the same. Eli was wrapped protectively in his arms, and he continued to stare unblinkingly through the spruce boughs into the northern woods. Mahihkan had not slept, and she knew that he would not sleep, until Eli was safely back in his body.

Morgan, on the other hand, was exhausted. She had been forced to run from life-threatening danger twice, and twice she'd almost been killed. Yes, she yearned for her brother to wake up. Yes, the thought of his death made her think more and more about her mother's death. Yes, she kept trying to think of how a soul might be drawn out of the moon stone. Yes, time was running out. But it was as though her mind said to her, "You're done." Whether she liked it or not. Morgan rested her head on Emily's shoulder, Emily reflexively put her arm around Morgan, and Morgan's eyelids—heavy as bricks—shut.

She fell asleep.

"Do you want to know how to save me?" a voice asked.

Morgan was holding the stone, from which she'd just taken off the strand of webbing, only now she wasn't on top of the mountain but deep within the northern woods. She looked up to see that the strand of web was dangling from an intricate maze of spiderwebs high above that connected twigs, branches, and treetops. The stone was warm in her hands, and gathering more heat every passing second. Soon it became so hot that she dropped it, and when it landed on the ground, a small fire erupted all around it, encasing the stone in flames.

"Yes, I want to know how to save you," she said, knowing that the stone was Eli, and his voice was coming from it. "That's all I want to know."

The single strand of webbing was suddenly joined by another, and then another, and the webbing continued to fall until it looked like sheets of rain in a thunderstorm. A million strands of web were dangling in front of her now, all coming from above, and they'd completely obstructed her view of the fire, of the stone, of Eli. She pushed the webs, thick and heavy, out of the way, from one side to another, as she waded forward, towards where she thought the fire had been. It felt as though she'd walked for hours when she finally came to the end of the webbing and into a clearing.

Morgan turned around and all she saw were strands of web, as many strands as there were hairs on her head. She backed away, deeper and deeper into the clearing, until everything came into view, and she realized that there hadn't been webs in front of her at all, but the sagging, leafy arms of a willow tree. The biggest willow tree that she'd ever seen.

"How do I save you?" she asked.

In response, a red light began to shine through the thick, sagging branches of the willow, as though the tree itself had a heart. The light grew brighter, and brighter, until the branches were pushed out of the way and Eli walked into the clearing, glowing like a setting sun.

He stopped there, locked eyes with Morgan, then looked back at the willow tree.

"With this," he said.

"Eli, what?" Morgan asked. "I don't . . . I don't understand. A willow tree? How will a willow tree save you?"

He didn't say anything, he just walked towards Morgan, and the closer he got, the warmer she felt. When he was close enough, she touched his skin, and it burned her fingertips.

"How do I save you?" she asked again.

"How do you stay calm?" he asked.

"Don't answer a question with a question," she said. "You're not my shrink."

"How do you stay calm?" he asked, this time slowly and quietly, as though trying to exude the calm he was speaking about.

Morgan took a deep breath in through her nose, exhaled through her mouth, and then her eyes fluttered open. She wasn't in the clearing anymore. Gone was her brother. Gone was the willow tree. She was back in the den where she and her companions had been hiding. The warm light that had come from Eli was now the sunrise creeping in through the spruce boughs Mahihkan had placed over the opening. She was lying on her side, facing Emily. Emily was already awake, looking deep into Morgan's eyes.

"Good morning," Emily said.

"Hi," Morgan said.

Emily put her hand on Morgan's cheek. "You were dreaming again, I could tell."

"I was dreaming," Morgan said.

"Any nightmares?" Emily asked.

"No. No nightmares," Morgan said.

"Good."

Emily smiled at Morgan, and it made Morgan feel warm again, as if she were back in the dream. Emily leaned forward, kissed Morgan on her cheek, and Morgan thought that maybe she hadn't woken up after all. She touched her fingertips against the place where Emily had kissed her, and then pinched herself just to make sure that she'd actually woken up.

"Ouch," she said.

Emily chuckled softly. "Was that okay?"

Morgan nodded. "Yes."

"So . . . what was your dream about?" Emily asked.

Morgan tried, again, to remember every detail, but again the details threatened to fade away. All she knew for certain was, just as before, the dream had felt so real. So real that Morgan thought maybe it *was* real. Maybe Eli had been with her, then and now. How else could he have shown her the stone in the first place? Because surely he had. It had been his voice saying her name. How else could he have given her enough clues to figure out that the hole in the sky was the entrance to the cave, that the flashes of lightning were the ocher drawings? Now, of all things, he'd shown her a willow tree.

"How do you stay calm?" he'd asked.

Her heart was racing from Emily's kiss. Morgan took a deep breath in through her nose, then exhaled through her mouth. Five seconds in, seven seconds out. Her heartbeat steadied.

If Eli had been right about those things, he had to have been right about what he'd just revealed to her. What *had* he revealed to her? Morgan shuffled over to her brother, who was secure in Mahihkan's arms. He turned Eli towards her, so that she could see his face. She pressed her fingertip against his skin, and watched to see how long the impression remained, a trick that she'd learned to test dehydration when googling how long a person could go without food or water. The shape of her fingertip was there for a second before Eli's skin eased back into place. A second didn't seem like much, but even one was too many. She ran her hands over his hair. She imagined it longer, the way it used to be before he cut it. She worried that he wouldn't get the chance to grow it out. His beautiful dark-olive skin had turned ghostly pale. He looked like a dead body set out for viewing at a wake.

"Why do you have to be so cryptic all the time?" she asked. But Morgan knew that his words—and the willow tree—were important, and that when the time came, she would know what to do. She would figure it out. She had to believe that, or else his soul would stay in the stone, away from his body, and in less than a day, he'd be gone forever.

Deep breath in, deep breath out.

THIRTEEN

First, there was the problem of the giant.

All night and into the morning he had walked by the entrance to the den on the same path. Morgan had slept through the night, but the others had heard him going north, and then south. One time, the wolf said, he had come towards the den and gone right past the opening, no more than five feet away. He didn't stop looking for them, for the moon stone, and it was clear that he never would. He wanted the stone back, and that meant they couldn't run anymore.

They had to figure out a way to beat him.

"Maybe we could bop him on the head and knock him out for long enough to escape," Arik said.

Emily snorted, trying to hold in laughter. "Bop him on the head, Arik? He's, like, ten feet tall."

"I *could* scurry up his back and hit him with something," Arik said, defensively. "My Bo staff, for example. My Bo staff is good for bopping."

"You do scurry really well," Morgan said.

"Thank you, Morgan."

"You'll only make him angry if you hit him with that stick," Mahihkan said. "The angrier he gets, the harder he'll be to defeat."

"So what's your big plan, then?" Morgan asked.

"We're going to have to kill him," the wolf said.

"Kill him?" Emily said. "Did you see what happened when I hit him with a hatchet? It was like he'd stubbed his toe! What do we have that could kill him?" Emily slapped herself on the forehead. "And I left the hatchet on the ground back there, anyway."

"So, to sum things up," Arik said, "we have my Bo staff, Morgan's slingshot, and your sharp teeth, Mahihkan."

"I told you that we had to kill him. I didn't say I knew how," Mahihkan said.

"What if we all went after him at once?" Arik suggested. "From all sides."

Mahihkan shook his head, and they fell silent, thinking. And after the silence had gone on for a long time, they heard, and felt, the giant walking towards them again from the south. They shuffled up to the spruce boughs to watch him walk by, as though seeing him would somehow spark a plan for how to kill him. All they saw was a massive, hairy beast that would laugh off a four-pronged attack. Mahihkan was right, though. Killing the giant was the only way; he wasn't going to leave them be. And if they were going to find a way to kill him, by the looks of Eli, it would have to be soon.

Morgan had felt some measure of hope upon waking that morning. She had another clue, just as the stone had been a clue in her first dream. But there were two parts of Eli in their hiding place—his body, clasped within Mahihkan's arms, and his soul, stuck in a rock resting on Morgan's lap—and no way to bring those two parts together unless they got rid of Mistapew. Here they were, trapped in a den with nowhere to go and nothing to do, and it was starting to feel less and less lucky that they'd found this den. In fact, it felt the opposite: monumentally *unlucky*. They would never have been here in the first place if that groundling mother hadn't come after them. Morgan began to wish that it had just swallowed them whole, to save her the heartbreak of losing Eli when they were so close to bringing him back.

Morgan suddenly gasped.

She was shushed quickly by the wolf—Mistapew was close by.

Emily, in a whisper, asked, "What's wrong?"

"Nothing's wrong," Morgan said. "I think I have a plan."

"Just like that?" Arik asked.

Morgan nodded. "Like a bop on the head."

She spent the next few minutes going over what had come to her. She wasn't sure how the others would react, but nobody protested. Nobody said that it was too crazy to work. Maybe because nobody could come up with anything better. And nobody refused to take part. In the end, it was all they had, and they were going to try. They had to wait until the sun was at its highest point, until the day was at its warmest. The timing had to be perfect for Morgan's plan to work because they'd only have one shot at it.

It was a tense morning. They tried to have breakfast, but nobody could stomach much. They watched the sky, trying to will the clouds off so that it would remain clear, so that the sun would shine down when it needed to. Everything depended on that. Whenever a cloud ambled across the sky and covered the sun, it was as though none of them could breathe until it continued on its way. They watched Mistapew as he continued to walk past the den— heading in this direction and then another—hoping that he might give up at some point, and render Morgan's plan unnecessary. But he didn't stop looking for them, so they made sure to know where he was, north or south, east or west, for when the time came.

Morgan told them all about her dream, as much as she could remember, to see if they could help her decipher it, because so far she'd not had much luck. Sure, there'd been the distraction of solving another problem—killing Mistapew—but four heads were better than one.

"I feel like the willow tree's significant," Morgan said, after recounting what she could of the dream. "What do you use a willow tree for?"

Emily was flummoxed, but Arik and Mahihkan exchanged a knowing look.

"The most common thing we'd use a willow tree for is to construct a sweat lodge," Mahihkan said.

"Yes, we use branches from it that are about the size of, oooohhhh"—she reached over and pinched at the fur around Mahihkan's chest, before the wolf slapped her hand away—"ribs. His ribs, not mine. Mine are much smaller, and branches the size of my ribs would never—"

"You've made your point, Arik," Mahihkan said, then worked to shrug off his annoyance at being prodded. "The branches are the skeleton of the sweat lodge. Hide is used to enclose the lodge and create a darkness inside it."

"Every ray of light needs to be blotted out," Arik added.

Morgan had learned a bit about sweat lodges at school, so she knew that heated rocks were placed inside the domed structure to generate the high temperature needed for the whole "sweat" thing to occur. That's about all she knew about them, but it was all she needed to know to be certain that's what the dream had been telling her. The stone had changed from glowing white to glowing red in her first dream, and in her second dream, it had become so hot that she dropped it, and it immediately became encased in fire.

"Sweat lodge rocks are heated in a fire," Morgan said, making this final connection out loud. She picked up the moon stone and held it out in front of her. "But if we heat this stone up and place it in a sweat lodge, how does Eli's soul get out of it?"

"Maybe it comes out with the steam?" Emily offered.

Morgan shrugged and nodded. "Steam *does* look ghostly," she admitted. "But then, if *that's* the case, okay, great, his soul's out of the stone . . . how does it go back inside his body?" She heard Eli's voice asking "How do you stay calm?" but she found no help in the words. Everything else was helpful, but what did her being calm have to do with anything? Of course she wasn't calm! Her brother was getting closer to death every second.

"He's told all of this to *you*, Morgan," Mahihkan said. Then he paused, and sighed, as though he didn't like this thought but accepted it. "Which means that *you* have to be in the sweat lodge. You and your brother."

"*Just* you and your brother," Arik clarified.

"*And* . . . ?" Morgan prompted, begging for an answer.

"And then you'll figure it out," Emily said to her, rubbing her back reassuringly.

As though in response to hearing Eli's question in her mind, Morgan took a deep breath in through her nose, then out through her mouth. Her breath trembled, then settled as much as could be expected.

"I'll figure it out," she said, glancing at Emily and trying to give her a confident smile—and trying to feel confident herself, trying to convince herself that, yes, she *would* figure it out.

They didn't speak of the dream after that, or much about anything at all, as though everybody else wanted to give Morgan the quiet she needed to find the last piece of the puzzle. So Morgan thought and thought and thought; they waited and waited and waited; and, no surprise, time crawled by. The sun gradually rose higher, as the sun is wont to do, and as it did the air warmed. Morgan could feel it from the shadowy den. And then at last the sun shone down brightly from the top of the sky. Mistapew had passed by no more than ten minutes ago, which meant, if he maintained the pattern he had followed all day, he would be back soon.

It was now or never.

Mahihkan pushed the spruce boughs out of the way. Eli was left on the ground with trepidation, but there wasn't a safer spot to put him. Morgan placed the moon stone beside him as if it might act as a guard against trouble, and the four emerged from the den, replacing the spruce boughs behind them to conceal the stone and the child. They positioned themselves in a straight line. Mahihkan walked through the clearing and then fifty yards south of it. Arik and Emily stood in the middle of the clearing, where the sun was shining and the northern woods were at their warmest. Morgan stood on the path north of the clearing, the crater and den to her left, and her slingshot raised, with a stone loaded and ready to fire. She looked back at Arik and Emily, and nodded. At her signal, they began to stomp their feet, trying to summon the groundlings.

Then Morgan waited. She waited until she felt tremors in the ground through her worn-out moccasins. They were faint, but present, and getting stronger with each passing second. She waited until she saw Mistapew approach, looking from left to right, scanning the area for the group that had stolen his possession.

He wouldn't need to look anymore.

"Hey! Mistapew!" she shouted. "Looking for me, you dumb, dirty ape?!"

At the sight of Morgan, the giant bellowed and broke into a run, heading right for her.

FOURTEEN

Morgan stood her ground, just as she had against Mason, just as she had against Muskwa, just as she had against the bully at school, and just as she'd learned to do when faced with darkness. Mistapew was closing in on her, his wide gait carrying him easily across the challenging, uneven terrain. Through underbrush, through reaching, dead branches from the trees, to get to Morgan. The giant's eyes looked so human it was unsettling, so angry it was terrifying, and she could feel her heart begin to race, but she was resolute, her hands steady, knowing that Eli's life hung in the balance.

"Come on," she whispered.

The rock was ready to fly towards its target, pinched securely between her thumb and index finger. Mistapew was close enough that the vibrations of his footsteps overtook the tremors from the groundlings, which, by now, Morgan hoped were circling Emily and Arik. So much of her plan was based on a hope that, under the same circumstances, what had happened before would happen again. Yes, the groundlings were there, she could feel them, but would they really circle Arik and Emily? Would they give way to their mother? What if they didn't? What then?

The giant was twenty yards away now. Morgan blew air out of her mouth, calming her jackhammering heart. *Thump. Thump. Thump. Thump. Thump. Thump. Thump.* Mistapew snarled. Ten yards away.

Now, Morgan thought, *do it now.*

She released the stone and it rocketed through the air, too fast for the giant to block it, though he tried. The projectile connected with his right eye, and he keeled over, clutching it. With Mistapew reeling for a moment, Morgan looked to see what was happening behind her in the clearing. She couldn't feel tremors. She couldn't see groundlings circling Arik and Emily. Arik was jumping up and down, waving her arms frantically, motioning Morgan towards the clearing. She looked like an air traffic controller after a hundred cups of coffee.

"He's up!" Emily shouted. "Let's go!"

Morgan turned around and saw that Mistapew had risen to his feet, looking angrier than ever. He took his hand away from his eye. There was blood streaming down his cheek. He roared. Morgan backed away. They were face to face in a showdown, each waiting for the other to move, but when Morgan felt the ground quake in a familiar, dreadful way, she knew she had to run. She was already worried that she'd not left enough space between her and the giant to be able to make it all the way to the clearing. Deciding that she needed more of a head start, she didn't fire another stone at Mistapew; instead, she threw her slingshot at him, and didn't wait to see how he reacted. She turned on her heel and hurried towards the clearing. But the slingshot must have done little to distract the giant, because as soon as she started running, she heard him giving chase behind her.

"Come and get me, you soul-stealing jerk!" she shouted, while sprinting so hard that her legs were burning.

Morgan imagined Eli was standing in the middle of the clearing, and if she didn't get there he'd float to the sky and she'd never see him again.

It gave her an extra gear.

She entered the clearing from the north at the same time Mahihkan entered the clearing from the south. Behind Morgan was Mistapew, his eye bleeding, enraged and desperate to get the moon stone back. Behind Mahihkan was a tidal wave of earth, reaching higher above the ground than the wolf himself. Morgan and Mahihkan ran towards each other at full steam, and as they got closer to one another, the hammering footsteps of the giant and the thundering tremors from the mother groundling converged into an earthquake that made the entire northern woods shudder.

The rolling dirt behind Mahihkan climbed higher and higher until Morgan could see the creature break through the surface. She hoped that Mistapew was too focused on her, too filled with anger, to stop. Arik and Emily rushed to safety. Mahihkan and Morgan were fifteen feet away from each other, then ten. She could feel the giant behind her. She could see the mouth of the mother groundling emerge, ready to devour whatever was in her path. Five feet. Mahihkan, at the last second, dove towards Morgan and tackled her out of the way. They hit the ground hard, and then were catapulted to the side as the groundling screamed before exploding from the dirt. Mistapew cried out in horror, shielding himself with his arms. But the act was in vain. The enormous creature took the giant into her mouth with one bite, pulling him into her stomach with her tongue in a fluid motion. Then she dove back under the surface, gone as quickly as she had come, leaving behind four weary travelers stunned into silence.

All of the northern woods seemed to be frozen from the shock of what had happened, and nobody moved for quite some time. Arik and Emily were on the ground on the opposite side of the large depression the mother groundling had left behind. Morgan was still protectively swaddled in Mahihkan's arms at the west edge of the clearing.

It wasn't until Arik bounced to her feet, clapped her hands, and said, "Well I, for one, could sure use some fermented cider!" that the others rose to their feet in somewhat of a daze.

"Did that," Morgan said, trying to catch her breath, "did that really just happen? Did it work?"

"Yes," Mahihkan said, "I think it did. I think we're safe."

He put his arm around her and gave her a reassuring squeeze. She moved some hair away from her face with a hand that would now not stop shaking, then looked up at the wolf. He smiled at her. Was that the first time she had seen him smile? It certainly was the first time he'd looked relieved. She smiled back, then buried her face in his fur and sighed the loudest and longest sigh ever.

"We've saved ourselves," Mahihkan said. "Now let's go save your brother."

FIFTEEN

Morgan, Emily, Arik, and Mahihkan met at the path at the north edge of the clearing, and headed to the den together in complete silence. What was there to say? They'd all just witnessed a huge creature being eaten by an even bigger creature, and two of them had narrowly escaped death in the process. Now they had to gather materials for a sweat lodge—which included locating a willow tree—and then find a spot where they could construct it, and build a fire that could heat the moon stone. Then Morgan had to sit in the structure with Eli and hope the steam from the stone would really be Eli's soul, and if it was, figure out how to get it back into his body before it floated off to the Happy Hunting Grounds.

Nothing came easily in the North Country.

Upon arriving at the den, the group was alarmed to find the spruce boughs shoved away clumsily, and inside, a bear on all fours was looming over Eli's sleeping body. It startled them, as they'd not seen much wildlife at all in the northern woods. Mahihkan urged the group to remain still so the bear wouldn't, in turn, become alarmed, as close to Eli's body as it was. It was a grizzly bear, Morgan thought, and probably a normal one. Not the sort that could walk and talk. It had no clothes on, and it was sniffing and snorting like a regular four-legged animal. It might have been better, however, to have found a bipedal bear in the den, because then they would have been able to reason with it. There was no reasoning with this bear, but something needed to be done, and quickly.

"What the heck's a bear doing in our hiding spot?" Morgan asked quietly.

"We were in its den," Mahihkan said. "It was simply a good place to hide."

"It seemed so at the moment, anyway," Arik said.

"You let us hide and sleep in a bear's den?" Emily asked.

"It was either that or get killed by the mother groundling, or Mistapew," Mahihkan said.

"Good point, good point," Emily said.

"Yeah, but what do we do now?" Morgan asked.

The animal didn't much care that four beings had stumbled upon its home; its interest was squarely focused on Eli. At the moment, it was curiously pushing his body from side to side.

"I guess we should've expected something like this," Arik said, "all things considered."

"Dude," Emily said, "*ya think?*" She sounded appalled.

Each time the bear swatted at Eli, testing to see whether he was alive or not, Morgan could hardly stand it.

"It's good that he *seems* dead, right?" Morgan asked. "If there's anything good about this."

"She probably has cubs around here somewhere," Mahihkan said, with growing concern.

"So what do we do?" Emily asked. "If we don't get him out of there by the time we get his soul back into his body, his body will have to go straight to the hospital."

"I know just what to do." Arik pulled out her Bo staff. Clearly, she was feeling particularly annoyed by the whole situation. "I've had about enough of furry beasts for one day." She looked at Mahihkan apologetically. "Except you, of course."

"You're also a furry beast, you know," Mahihkan grumbled.

Arik ignored the comment and marched up to the den with footsteps as loud as she could muster.

"Hey! You! Grizzly!" she shouted.

The grizzly abandoned Eli and, with a loud grunt, met Arik at the mouth of its den. It opened its mouth to roar, but before it could, Arik hit it on the nose with her Bo staff.

"That's enough from you," she said. "Now go on."

Arik gave the bear another bonk on the snout, and it retreated deep into its den, leaving Eli alone.

"Wow, that was . . . unexpected," Emily said.

"No kidding," Morgan agreed.

Before the grizzly could think about coming back, Mahihkan gathered up Eli, Morgan retrieved the moon stone, and they hastened out of the den.

They headed south. Morgan knew there was a lot of ground to cover and not much wiggle room before, back on earth, Katie and James would wake up. It wasn't her main concern, but if they could bring Eli to life and return to the secret room before their foster parents got out of bed, it would be a bonus.

They walked around the clearing this time, not through it, because nobody wanted to encounter more groundlings. And because none of them, from their journey north, could recall seeing a spot that would offer enough room to build a lodge, they didn't return to the path. Instead they opted for a new route, to see parts of the northern woods they hadn't seen yet.

The return trek went more quickly, even without a path. As before, Mahihkan carried Eli. And not having to pull him on a sled, which had proved to be difficult even with a trail, more than made up for having to forge their way through the bush. But as the day wore on and the sun dipped, giving way to dusk, the northern woods they hadn't seen began to look exactly like the northern woods they had seen. Thick, tall dead trees with their naked branches like old fingers. Dried-out underbrush that scratched at their skin like barbed wire. Bush devoid of any green, looking more like tumbleweed. Gray all around, from the groundlings sucking the life out of everything. And what scared Morgan was that, by the light of the moon stone, Eli's skin looked as if it were painted from the same color palette.

She was losing him.

When night fell, the northern woods were cloaked in black. Using one torch to guide them, and with great desperation, they settled on an area. There was room for just a small sweat lodge, but they reasoned that because only Morgan needed to sit in it, and Eli could lie curled around the fire where the moon stone would be placed, it was good enough. The fear was that if they walked farther and found nothing, the fourth day would come upon them, and by then it would certainly be too late. Eli needed water desperately to survive.

Eli's breath had grown shallow, his skin dry. Morgan again touched his cheek and watched how long it took for his skin to fall back in place. It seemed as though his skin stayed right where it was, the shape of her fingertip stuck there as though she'd pressed down on playdough.

The first thing they did was build a small fire atop a bed of rocks and dirt, not wanting to risk summoning the groundlings. Later, to heat the moon stone, they would build up the same fire, but for now it served to light the clearing. The concern was how much hide there was. They already had deer skin for the tent, but would it be enough to cover every inch of the dome so that no air could get in or out? Morgan was worried. What if they had to catch a deer? In the southern woods, it wouldn't have been a problem; game was plentiful there, and had been for years. But here, they'd only seen one bear.

Mahihkan, who would leave nothing to chance when it came to Eli's safety, thought what they had was sufficient, and Arik agreed. So, that was a big relief to everyone.

The tent poles were not going to help build the sweat lodge, though.

"You *do* need willow branches," Arik insisted. "It's the

only thing that'll work. You dreamed of the willow tree for a reason."

"Dreaming of one might've been appropriate. I don't recall seeing one in the years I've roamed these woods," Mahihkan said.

"I mean, have you roamed *all* these woods?" Emily asked.

"Either way, we don't have a choice," Morgan said. "If we don't find willow branches, there's no sweat lodge, and if there's no sweat lodge . . ."

"Couldn't we just heat the rock and put water on it and catch his soul out in the open?" Emily asked.

"No," Morgan said. "I know that if he showed me the willow tree, it means nothing will work without one. And I don't think he would've told me about willow branches unless there was a willow tree *somewhere* around here."

"I suppose I haven't roamed *every* inch of these woods," Mahihkan admitted, forcing some hope into the situation.

"Okay, so, Morgan and I will go find a willow tree," Emily said.

"We'll go find a willow tree," Morgan agreed. Then she picked up the moon stone and held it with both her hands, as though it were as fragile as an egg. She walked over to Mahihkan and handed it to him. He took it, with just as much care as Morgan had shown. "Start heating it up now, so that when we come back with the branches, it'll be ready."

"I will have it ready," Mahihkan assured her.

"I'll take out the sinew that's stitching the pieces of hide together to make the tent. Then I can lay them all out and have them ready to place over the branches," Arik said.

"Ekosani," Morgan said to the other three, "for every-thing."

"Níwakomakanak," was all Arik said.

Morgan grabbed a piece of burning wood from the fire to use as a torch, took Emily's hand, and they started on their search.

"What's a willow tree look like, anyway?" Emily asked. "Is it the one with the droopy leaves that kind of look like vines?"

"Yeah," Morgan said. "When it's alive, anyway. I don't know about when it's dead, like all the other trees that are out here."

"I guess even if it's dead it'll have kind of the same shape."

Morgan pictured the tree she'd seen in her dream. "The branches were like lightning bolts frozen in time, and instead of leaves it looked like a head of long, tattered hair. When we see that, we've found the tree."

"Look who's still a poet," Emily said.

"Maybe next assignment Mrs. Edwards will give me more than a B+," Morgan said. "Talk about bad kinds of *B*s."

"You've got brains and beauty, too, Morg."

"Thanks, Houldsy."

Then they fell silent, and the only sounds were their footsteps trudging through the woods, broken branches underfoot, the whip of dead grass against their shins.

"Do you want to talk about this morning?" Emily asked.

"I nodded, didn't I?" Morgan said. "You asked if kissing me was okay, and I nodded. Nodding means yes, not no. I think I actually said yes, too."

"I was just worried that . . ."

"You sound like me right now," Morgan said. "Don't worry, it's not going to be some 'unspoken thing' that we ignore forever."

"Just when I thought I couldn't like you more, you quote Star-Lord and Gamora from *Guardians of the Galaxy*," Emily said, squeezing Morgan's hand.

"Just when I thought I couldn't like *you* more, you come to another world with me and help save my brother's life," Morgan said, squeezing her hand back.

They laughed, they glanced at each other, there was another few seconds of silence, and then Emily let out a deep breath. A Morgan-like breath. As though she was exhaling all the worry she'd been feeling.

"Okay," Emily said as they walked farther away from the clearing, the fire, and deeper into the dark of the northern woods, "let's go find this tree."

SIXTEEN

As the girls made their way farther into the woods, Mahihkan stoked the fire to heat the moon stone. While the fire would make it easy for Morgan and Emily to find their way back, they also left a trail of breadcrumbs behind, just to be sure they wouldn't get lost—a broken twig, a trampled-over bush, a stick thrust into the dirt. If their search somehow took them far enough away that they lost the firelight, they could follow these hints.

They walked to the west, towards the mountains. Morgan had a hunch they'd be more likely to find a willow tree in this direction: the forest would gradually thin out as they got closer to the mountains, she thought, and willows needed more space than other trees, so that's where they'd be. But as the minutes passed, she started to question the decision. Nothing was changing about the forest, and they weren't going to walk as far as the mountains anyway. If they did, they wouldn't get back before morning.

The fire, by now, would undoubtedly be raging, and she hoped that the moon stone was changing from glowing white to a bright red.

"Come on, Eli," Morgan whispered. "Help me."

She stopped walking and turned around in a full circle, holding out the torch to light the area, but she saw nothing.

"Maybe you should ask Creator, not Eli," Emily said. "That's the name you use, right?"

"That's . . ." Morgan was going to say that the idea was stupid, but she knew there was, in fact, a Creator. Well, she'd seen Creator's hands, anyway, as they lifted Ochek to the stars. And she had heard the voice, too. "Creator probably has more important things to do."

"Do you think Creator had more important things to do when he caught Ochek in midair?" Emily asked.

"That's fair," Morgan said.

She tried to remember how she'd seen Eli pray when he'd talked to Creator. She pictured him as though he were there. He would close his eyes, lay tobacco down on the earth, then whisper something to Creator. Simple.

Morgan patted at both of her pockets, and found the tobacco tie that Muskwa had given her. She heard his voice. *Creator keep you safe.* Could Creator also guide them?

"Doesn't hurt to try, right? So, uhhh, I'll just . . ."

Morgan handed Emily the torch, then went down on her knees. She opened the tobacco tie, and sprinkled the sacred medicine across the ground. *How do you talk to Creator? What do you say?* she thought. She tried to remember what Eli said when he prayed, what Oho said when they prayed, how every human and animal being had prayed in front of her. She realized that they all did it differently, but the common thing was that they spoke from the heart.

Morgan cleared her throat, closed her eyes, and began to pray.

"Tansi, Creator. It's me, Morgan. We met by the sequoia tree, in case you forgot. Thanks for catching Ochek, by the way. That was awesome. Anyway, I know you're busy, but I wanted to know if you could help me out. See, my brother, Eli, is dying. That stupid giant took his soul and, well, I guess you probably know what's happened because you know everything. We've come so far to get here. We're so close to getting him back, and I just need one little thing. Can you show me and Emily where a willow tree is? Pretty random, right? But I need the branches so I can build a sweat lodge and . . . it's complicated, but yeah, if I can't build the sweat lodge then I can't put Eli's soul back in his body. Could you show me where one is? Or just, like, point me in the right direction? Ummm, okay, I guess that's it. Thank you. Ekosani."

Morgan opened her eyes and got to her feet. She stood next to Emily, waiting. Waiting for what, she didn't know. Would a big, glowing hand descend upon the northern woods and literally point her in the right direction? Would a lightning bolt, like the shape of the branches of the willow tree, something super symbolic, strike the ground and set a willow tree on fire, showing them where one was? *But also burning it, so that would suck,* Morgan thought. A thousand different scenarios played over in her brain. A minute passed. Then another. As more time passed, Emily glanced over at Morgan more frequently, silently asking her to start walking again.

They couldn't stand there all night.

Morgan kept scanning the woods for something, anything, that might be Creator's answer to her prayers, but nothing came. It was just as gray, just as dead, as it was before. The only difference was the warm light and the shadows, cast by the torch. The shadows worked hard to give life to the northern woods, dancing across the ground, but it was an illusion.

"We should keep going," Emily said carefully, as though not wanting to make Morgan feel like she'd failed.

Of course, she hadn't failed. Creator didn't answer every prayer. But Morgan felt that way, and tried to shake off the disappointment.

"Yeah, it's gotta be out there somewhere," Morgan said.

She took a step, ready to continue the willow tree quest, but when she took that step, she stopped. There was something in the distance. A movement. There, then gone. But there.

"What is it?" Emily asked.

"I just . . ." Morgan focused on the spot, and shone her torch in that direction. "I thought I saw something."

"Something like what?"

Morgan waited to see it again. It was a silhouette. Or maybe, she conceded, a shadow moving from the torch's shifting light.

"Nothing," she said. "It was . . ."

But there it was again. A dark figure. She moved the torch from side to side, and while every other shadow moved with the light, the silhouette turned towards her and Emily, as if watching them.

"Do you see that?"

"Yes, it's right there." Emily pointed at it. "What is it? You don't think it's another northern woods creature, do you? I mean, Creator wouldn't answer your prayer with a creepy shadow thing. Right?"

The silhouette made a movement, as if gesturing for the two of them to follow it, then disappeared into the darkness, out of reach of the torchlight.

"If a creepy shadow thing is going to lead us to the willow tree, then why not?" Morgan said. "Let's go."

They walked after it.

"Oh god," Emily said, "three days ago I was thinking about what kind of cereal I was going to have for breakfast, and now I'm following a shadow through a dead forest looking for a tree so you can release a soul from a stone."

"Just a regular day in the North Country," Morgan said.

The figure was quick, and didn't so much walk as glide over the terrain. Morgan and Eli worked to keep pace. They, unlike the shadow, had to deal with the underbrush. But they kept up, and soon enough it led them into an open area that, Morgan thought, would have served nicely for the sweat lodge and fire, but of course it was too late for that.

In the middle of the clearing, with the moon shining down on it like a spotlight, was a willow tree, just like the one from her dream.

A trunk broke off into jagged branches that became thinner the farther out they reached. Dried-out leaves hung from twigs, like scraggly hair, and reached to the ground. The shadowy figure paused in front of the tree, turned towards the girls, held its position for a few seconds, and then walked into the leaves. Morgan and Emily ran over to where it had been, but the silhouette had disappeared completely, leaving the girls standing underneath the willow tree.

They didn't discuss where the figure had gone, or who had sent it to them. Morgan wondered to herself if it had been Eli, finding a way to reach her one last time, or if Creator had sent a guide, or maybe even both. Whatever the answer, they broke off as many rib-sized branches as they could carry, tied them together with strips of cloth torn from their shirts, and made their way back to the fire, carrying the surprisingly light bundles on their shoulders.

When they got back to the clearing, Arik had laid out all the hide and sinew, ready to repurpose it as coverings for the sweat lodge. The fire was blazing, reaching towards the night sky, and the stone was bright red, like a blood moon, and ready for the sweat. The girls plunked down the wood near the hide. They had everything they needed.

Now it had to work.

SEVENTEEN

The frame of the sweat lodge was difficult to assemble because the wood was too firm. Willow branches were used for their flexibility, but it turned out that dead willow branches weren't all that flexible. They decided to use shorter, stronger branches, and tie them together end to end to create the curve needed. The branches met at the top, where they were joined together with sinew, then more were used horizontally to make the structure sturdy. When they were done, they had a dome that would serve their purpose, small and strong. To complete the lodge, they covered it in deer hides, and tied one hide to the other so no section would fall away and let out smoke or heat. If something like that happened at the wrong time, Eli's soul could float off to the Happy Hunting Grounds. There were more than enough hides to cover every inch of the lodge, and the animal beings made sure that the entrance faced east.

"Why does it have to face east?" Emily asked. "Is that important?"

"Ehe," Arik said. "The entrance faces east, where the sun rises, because if the sun didn't rise there would be no life."

"Like in the northern woods," Morgan said.

"Exactly, like in the northern woods," Arik said. "But even still, it's tradition. And the sun always rises."

With the lodge standing, Mahihkan sprinkled tobacco into the fire, where the moon stone was bright red, engulfed by flames. Then, he made a trail with the sacred medicine from the fire all the way into the lodge.

"We do this," he said while on his way to the lodge, perhaps anticipating more questions, "because the sweat lodge is the womb of mother earth."

"That's why the willow branches are like ribs," Morgan said. "It's like inside her torso or whatever."

"That's right," the wolf said. "We leave a line of tobacco from the fire to the womb like an umbilical cord, which gives life just as the sun does."

An image from her dream, of the moon stone being lowered into her hands by a single strand of the spider's web, flashed into Morgan's mind.

The last thing was to smudge the sweat lodge. Morgan was given that task, because she would be the only one of the four inside. Arik had a bundle of sage, an eagle feather, and a bowl in her pack, and she gave them to Morgan. Morgan lit the sage, watching as a small fire erupted from the medicine, then blew it out gently. Smoke rose from the bowl, and Morgan feathered it over every inch of the lodge's walls.

"What now?" Morgan asked, emerging from the lodge and handing Arik the smudge bowl.

"You're anxious," Mahihkan said.

"Of course I am," she said. "You see the same Eli, right? I want to get him back."

"We all do, but we need to do this in a good way. Eli would agree, wouldn't he?"

"Yes," Morgan muttered.

"Here." Arik handed Morgan the rest of her sage. "When you're in the lodge with Eli, before you start to pray, you need to say 'All my relations.' Place this sage on the rock and thank it."

"Thank it for what?" Morgan asked.

"For what you feel you need to thank it for," Arik said. "Whatever comes to your heart."

"And then do I pour the water on the stone?"

"Yes, while you pray," Mahihkan said.

"It'll be hot in there, even with just one stone," Arik said. "Remember that sweat is negative energy leaving your body."

"Muskwa said that to me about crying," Morgan said. "He said crying is letting all the bad things out of your body."

"Muskwa," Mahihkan said, "is a wise bear."

"You're getting soft in your old age," Morgan teased.

The wolf growled, short and sharp.

"Or not," she added hastily.

Morgan stood at the entrance with sage clasped in one hand and a water pouch in the other, which held fresh water from the stream by Mistapew's home. Mahihkan carried Eli into the lodge and placed him down, curled in the center.

"Well, I guess this is it," Morgan said.

"Good luck," Emily said, giving Morgan a prolonged hug. "I wish I could go in there, for moral support or whatever."

"I know."

"Bring him back, Morgan," Mahihkan said.

"Yes, please do," Arik said. "Misewa wouldn't be the same without the boy."

"Neither would I," Morgan said.

She ducked into the lodge and sat on the north side, to the right of the entrance. Her palms were sweating, and it wasn't even hot yet. She kept rubbing them against her pants. And she stared at Eli's limp body. A couple of days ago, he'd looked as though he were sleeping; now it was as if they'd put a corpse into the structure with her.

Mahihkan placed the moon stone in the middle of the lodge beside Eli, then backed away. Arik and Emily closed the flap, and Morgan was awash in the stone's sunset-colored light and its intense heat. Eli used to talk about going into a sweat with thirteen "grandfathers" (the name he'd learned for the stones), and Morgan couldn't imagine that. One was enough for her. Within seconds she felt sweat dripping down her face.

"All my relations."

Now offer sage, Morgan thought, remembering the instructions she'd been given.

She placed the sage on the rock and it instantly burst into flame. When the fire died out, smoke rose from it and gathered at the top of the lodge, trapped there. Morgan considered this a test of the dome's construction, and it had been made well.

"Ekosani, stone," she said, "for housing my little brother's soul. For keeping it safe."

As she spoke, she felt wetness curling over her cheeks, slipping over her lips—not just sweat, but tears. Tears for Eli. Tears for her mother, who Morgan pictured exactly the way she'd appeared in her dreams. Were those dreams real? Had her mother been trying to reach her, like Eli had? Her crying turned to sobbing, but as the seconds passed, so too did the sadness. In its place was gratefulness. If all the dreams with her mother had somehow been real, then she was grateful that they'd spent that time together.

But Morgan didn't want dreams with Eli. She wanted Eli. Period. She couldn't save her mother, but she could still save him. Morgan closed her eyes.

"Creator," she said. "It's me again. I know you literally just helped me already tonight, but I've got one more thing to ask. Since you showed me where the willow tree was—if that was you, which it probably was—then you'll do this one last thing, right? I don't need your help pouring water on this stone. I can handle that part. I need you to show me what to do. Please show me what to do to get my brother back in his body. Please. I'll do anything. I can't have just met him, only to lose him so soon. He can't die after everything we've been through together. Please do this for me. I won't ask for anything again. Ekosani."

Morgan raised the pouch and tilted it to the side. Water streamed from within it and splashed with a hiss against the red-hot stone. Steam rose from the stone and billowed into the air, collecting in a pool of smoke under the ceiling of the lodge. She inspected the steam thoroughly, but couldn't see anything that looked like a soul. She noticed, however, that the stone had begun to glow white again.

"Come on," she whispered. "Come on, Eli. You're in there. I know you are."

Then she saw it. A ghostly figure rose from the moon stone. Morgan could see the suggestion of arms and a head. It seemed to look at her, then upward, towards the sky. Where the Happy Hunting Grounds were. It didn't want to stay on Askí. It wanted to go back to the sky, to the stars, where Ochek was. There wasn't much time. It rose higher, and the cloud of smoke above broke apart as though to make way for it. Light shone down on the soul, on Morgan, on the stone. It opened through the hide like another portal. Morgan's body began to shake from panic. Her breath became short and shallow. Her heart pounded to get out of her chest, as though it wanted to join Eli's soul on its journey to heaven.

thump thump thump thump thump thump thump

Not now, Morgan thought. *Not now.*

She took a deep breath in through her nose, closing her eyes for a moment, allowing herself five seconds to help quiet her mind so she could think clearly. She felt hot air slide down her throat and into her chest, and the heat stayed there, but it wasn't the same heat she'd felt so often when there was panic or anger.

It was calm.

It was peace.

It was sitting on the bank of a river and watching the swift water run past. It was walking through the southern woods and breathing in the fresh air. It was leaning against a Great Bear on the Barren Grounds and staring up at the sky, at a constellation made to honor a fallen hero. It was a dream in a small room with a mother, asking her daughter not to forget herself. *Kiskisitotaso*. It was the life she felt in her mother, in her brother, when there didn't seem to be any life left.

It was joy.

It was hope.

Morgan knew, when she opened her eyes and saw the hazy figure gone, that Eli hadn't been pulled to the Happy Hunting Grounds, but rather, she had breathed him in.

His soul was holding her heart.

And she knew what she had to do.

How do you stay calm?

Morgan, keeping the breath held in, crawled over to Eli's body and turned him onto his back. She lifted his head and placed it onto her lap. She leaned over until her face was inches from his, then let the breath out slowly through her mouth. A white vapor trail led from her mouth into his nostrils, and Eli breathed in until all trace of his soul was gone from Morgan.

She combed his hair with her fingers. She placed her other hand on his cheek. He was still cold and clammy, still pale, his breath still shallow.

"Wake up," Morgan whispered.

She watched, and felt, for any sign that he was with her again. A flickering eyelid. A groan, as though he'd been forced out of a long sleep. A gasp for air. Warm, flushed skin. A quickened heartbeat. Anything.

"Wake up, kid, please."

A raspy breath came from Eli. A light cough. He raised his arm and held his hand to his throat. His eyelids fluttered, then opened. They locked eyes. A tear landed on Eli's nose, then slid down his face.

"Stop," he said in a whisper, his voice hoarse, "calling me . . . kid."

Morgan laughed. She lifted Eli up and wrapped her arms around him. His soul had left her chest but it was in the right place, and she felt no less warmth, no less hope, and no less joy.

"Eli," she said, "I promise that I'll never call you kid again."

EIGHTEEN

Morgan poured a little of the water into Eli's mouth, then opened the flap to give him some air. The other three had been waiting right outside the lodge, desperate to see if the ceremony had worked or not, and when Morgan pushed the flap open they were so close it startled her. After catching her breath, she smiled, which told Emily and the animal beings all they needed to know.

"I just want to give him some time before bringing him out," she said, and the others understood.

The chilly air from the northern woods overtook the heat within the sweat lodge quickly, and when Eli started to shiver, Morgan took off her hoodie and placed it over his body. She gave him another sip of water, which he swallowed.

"What happened?" he asked, his voice already sounding stronger.

"What do you remember?" she asked.

"I followed you through the portal," he said. "You were lying down in front of the Great Tree. You'd been crying,

I think. You were really upset. I was mad that you'd gone to Askí without me, but when I saw you, I wasn't mad anymore. I just wanted to be there for you. So I lay down with you and fell asleep. And then, I don't know. I had a dream. It was one of those dreams that last forever, that feel so real. Like, when you wake up and you're surprised it *wasn't* real. You know?"

"Yeah," Morgan said, "I know."

"You were in it. You were on a mountaintop and there was this, like, portal in the sky. I was . . ." Eli closed his eyes, trying to recall. "I was in your arms. You were holding me in your arms. There was a tree, there was . . ." Eli shook his head and started to rub his temples. It looked as though it hurt too much to think, and Morgan didn't need to hear it anyway. She'd dreamed the same dreams.

"It's okay," she said. "I'll fill you in on everything you missed."

"Missed?" Eli said, and with some effort he propped himself up on his elbows. He licked his lips, still dry from days without water, then his stomach grumbled. "I'm so hungry."

"That's not surprising. Lucky for you, we've got some pimíhkán."

Morgan helped him to his feet. He wobbled a bit, and she steadied him.

"Pimíhkán?" Eli said. "Did we go somewhere?"

"Don't we always?" Morgan chuckled. "This is us we're talking about. Only . . . usually you aren't sleeping the whole time. Luckily, there's still a bit of a walk ahead of us."

"Who's we?" he asked. "You said 'we've got some pimíhkán.' Is Arik here?"

Eli and Morgan emerged from the sweat lodge. It was dark out. The raging fire, stoked to heat the rock, had been allowed to dwindle. Morgan's eyes had to adjust to the darkness, and if she hadn't already known who they were, she wouldn't have been able to make out the three shadowy beings standing around the fire, waiting for them.

"See for yourself," Morgan said.

Eli rubbed his eyes and peered into the dark.

"Mahihkan!" he cried at last. And despite how weak he must have felt, he rushed towards the wolf and they flung their arms around each other. "Is it really you? Are you really here?" he asked, his voice muffled by fur.

"It's really me, Eli," Mahihkan said. "It's really me, and you, thank Creator, are really here, too."

"Hmmph," Arik said. And she turned, with a sly grin, to Emily and Morgan. "Who are we, unimportant beings?"

"You know, on earth, we'd ask if we were chopped liver," Emily said.

"Yeah, like, 'What am I, chopped liver?'" Morgan said.

"Why would I ask if I was chopped liver?" Arik asked. "I think chopped liver is yummy. I'd love to be called chopped liver. Well, not if somebody wanted to eat me. Then I'd want to be something disgusting."

So while Eli and Mahihkan embraced, Emily and Morgan laughed, and Arik stood there, hands on her hips, with a confused look on her face until Morgan explained the figure of speech.

They ate by the fire. More specifically, everybody watched Eli eat by the fire as they all gave him the rest of their pimíhkán, knowing that by morning they'd be at the Great Tree and safely out of the northern woods.

"I don't mind walking through the Barren Grounds with a grumbling tummy as long as you're alive and well," Arik had said to Eli while handing him her rations. "Anyway, I'm—"

"More of a nut person, yourself," Morgan said.

"You know me so well." Arik blushed, then darted off into the woods, but not so far away that they couldn't see or hear her. "In fact, I'm going to find a nut or two right now, and you can eat some if you like, Eli, if the pimíhkán isn't enough."

"Thanks," Eli said. "I'm good."

"It'd be a dry nut, anyway," Emily warned. "There's nothing alive in these woods but some stuff by a stream around that giant's cave."

"Giant?" Eli repeated. "You mean Mistapew?"

"Yeah, that big furry guy," Emily said.

"I can't believe we're in the northern woods," Eli said.

"Boy, when you hear everything, that's going to be the *easiest* part to believe," Mahihkan said.

"You mean like how it's pretty much impossible that you're alive?"

"Trust me, Eli," the wolf said, "me being alive is far more believable than you sitting with us now. The river washed me away to the east, to World's End. I was nursed back to health by some pisiskowak there, and I've lived in these woods ever since. There's nothing remarkable about it."

"World's End?" Eli said.

"You sound so much like Arik right now," Morgan said, "asking what everything is. I love it."

"Hey!" Arik called out from an overhanging branch, foraging for whatever nuts she could find. "I heard that."

"World's End," Mahihkan said. "The woods to the east, where the trees disappear against the horizon, where the sun is born every day. There's a village there named Ministik."

The wolf went on to describe the woods, the village, and the pisiskowak, animal beings, living within it. Eli had a look of wonder on his face, and Morgan, watching him, did too, as though it was catching. But her wonder came from the fact that her brother was alive and well, against all odds, and that she could see the happiness Askí brought him. One day soon, they would be off on another adventure, and she couldn't wait. She had thought for awhile that she might never go on another journey with Eli. And, even better, Emily could now come with them.

"So, you're sure Mason is dead?" Eli asked, after the wolf had finished his story.

"Ehe," Mahihkan said. "Believe me. There was no life left in him."

"Dead as a tree in the northern woods!" Arik jumped down into the clearing from a tree, startling the other four. Mahihkan clutched his chest and had to catch his breath. "Oh ho! Who's afraid, big bad wolf?!"

Emily started to laugh hysterically.

"What? What did I say?" Arik said.

"Oh, it's just that—"

"Ah!" Morgan shook her head at Emily with an index finger raised. "This turns into a rabbit hole, trust me. We'll just bring 'The Three Little Pigs' next time we come, okay?"

"What's this about rabbit holes and kokoswak?" Arik asked. "You aren't keeping secrets from me, are you? Because I won't share my nuts if you are."

"Kokoswak means pigs," Eli said to both Morgan and Emily.

"I even missed you explaining everything to me," Morgan said to Eli. "And you can keep your nuts, Arik. I think I'd rather be hungry."

Arik shoved a handful into her mouth and her cheeks puffed out, which made everybody laugh again, even Mahihkan.

"Suit yourself," Arik mumbled.

"Wait a minute," Eli said. "You've gone on some kind of journey, with me sleeping, into a place that I thought was forbidden, and it's been long enough that you've missed things about me." Eli placed his bowl of pimíhkán on the ground. "How long was I unconscious for? What happened?"

Morgan looked at Arik for some help, but the squirrel just shrugged. Mahihkan and Emily didn't say anything to her either when she looked to them. They were leaving this answer for her.

"I . . . look, Eli . . . maybe you should wait. You've been back for what, half an hour?"

"I know you're trying to protect me, and I appreciate it," he said, "but you don't have to. I can take it, and I want to know."

Morgan thought of everything Eli had been through, his body and his soul.

"Yeah, I guess you *can* take it," she conceded.

And so, in front of the fire, with the other three listening as though they'd not just been through it all, Morgan told Eli the story of how they found his soul, and how it was placed back into his body. No detail was spared. Morgan did her best to recall every moment, and when something wasn't clear, Eli asked. When she forgot something, even the smallest thing, like how they'd covered the opening of the bear's den, Arik or Emily or Mahihkan would politely interrupt, and then Morgan would carry on. The story went on for a long while, because a lot had happened in three days, but Morgan eventually finished, and then waited for Eli's reaction.

He'd left a spoonful of pimíhkán in his bowl, and he finished it now, then sat thoughtfully before stating, "So you guys killed Mistapew."

"I mean, yeah," Emily said. "I guess we did."

"But we kind of had to," Morgan said.

"He *did* trap you inside a stone," Arik said.

"But there's more of them, right?" Morgan asked desperately, suddenly worried that they'd made bigfoot extinct. "Didn't you say once that people had seen Mistapew around your community, Eli?"

"Yeah, right around my grandpa's trapline," Eli said. "Somebody even took a video of it once from across the river."

"Oh, thank god," Morgan said.

"I can't believe Mistapew lived in these woods for hundreds of years and now he's . . . gone," Eli said with more than a hint of sadness.

"Why do you care?" Emily asked. "The dude took your soul and you almost died."

"*I* know what a dude is," Arik said proudly.

"If Eli didn't care for even the worst of us," Mahihkan stood up, "I wouldn't be here today." He walked over to Eli. "And I wouldn't be able to keep watch while you get some rest before the last of our journey, Assini Awasis."

"What does Assini Awasis mean?" Morgan asked.

"Stone Child," Eli said.

NINETEEN

The sweat lodge was only big enough for two people, but that night four of them—Arik, Eli, Morgan, and Emily—snuggled up all together inside. The fifth member of their group—Mahihkan—remained outside, sitting by the fire, forever scanning the northern woods for danger. The wolf had not rested for one minute since saving Arik, Morgan, and Emily from the groundlings, and he wouldn't allow himself a break until he knew the four were safe, back at the Great Tree, where all of this had begun.

Morgan had fallen asleep nestled up to Emily, and quickly fell into a dream where she was walking through a field of snow towards a bungalow on the outskirts of a forest. There was one window on the side of the house that faced her, and a light shone from within. Morgan walked towards the light. Once there, she saw her mother, Jenny Trout, gently rocking back and forth with Morgan, just a toddler, cradled in her arms. The child was smiling. Jenny was crying. She was humming a song, but teenage Morgan couldn't hear it.

Jenny's head jerked up, looking away from her daughter, towards the door. A man and a woman entered the room. One of them took the girl while the other held Jenny back. In the struggle, the side table was knocked over, and a lamp crashed against the ground. The room was bathed in black.

Jenny stood in the room, in the dark, and Morgan was left banging on the window from the outside. But there was no sound from Morgan's palm slapping against the glass. There was no sound when Morgan opened her mouth and screamed so hard that her throat and chest hurt. Jenny Trout dissolved into thin air, and Morgan was left wondering what the dream meant, what her mother was trying to tell her.

Nothing, that's what, she thought.

On this journey together, Eli had been sending Morgan clues, and though they'd been puzzling, he had been able to show her things that Morgan understood. Eli was alive. Jenny Trout was not, and to Morgan, the dream meant exactly that. That's why she couldn't get inside the room. That's why she couldn't make a sound, or scream for those two people to stop, to not take her younger self away.

Darkness.

The window was gone, and the house was gone with it. Morgan wasn't standing in the snow. She couldn't feel the damp cold seeping into her moccasin from the hole she'd worn into it. She couldn't feel the snow sting against her skin from the blizzard raging around her. There was still darkness, but she felt warmth. She could feel the sticky heat inside the sweat lodge. She could feel Emily's body pressed against her back, Emily's arm wrapped around her. Her head was resting on Emily's other arm. She could feel Arik sprawled out over the humans' legs. She could feel Eli's body held tight within her arms. She could feel his breath, soothing against her skin. She opened her eyes, and saw Eli sleeping soundly. She could feel his soul. It was inside his body but holding her heart. She needed that feeling, to feel something other than loss. There, right in front of her, was something she'd gained. She leaned forward and kissed him on the forehead. He opened his eyes.

"Morning," she said.

"Morning." His voice was croaky, but not from a dry throat. It was croaky from sleep, from waking up when his body wanted to keep resting. She wished that he could, but Morgan knew their time on Askí had to come to an end very soon. Katie and James would be waking up any minute. Maybe they already had. But Morgan was too relieved to worry much about that, about what they'd say if she and Eli came down from their secret room, with a friend, no less. A school-night secret-room sleepover? Whatever. They'd used worse excuses.

"You know," she said, "I have a whole new appreciation for you waking up now."

"As long as you don't make a habit of waking me up when I'm tired," he said.

"Sorry!" She chuckled. "But we'd better get moving. This is the fourth day we've been here, and we only had three and a half."

"It'll be morning when we get home?" Eli said.

"Yeah, if my Misewa Math isn't wrong, and it usually isn't," Morgan said. "Ready to go?"

"Yes," he said. "I'm ready."

When everybody was awake, they packed up and left for the Great Tree. They had no food, so there was no breakfast, and this saved time. With Eli walking, they could quicken their pace, as well.

They'd left while it was still dark, and by the time the sun had risen in the east, with its light filtering into the northern woods, the Great Tree wasn't that far off. Mahihkan led the way, with Arik and Emily trailing behind him, and Morgan and Eli behind the others. The wolf was quiet, looking back only every once in a while to make sure Eli was okay.

"I think he'd follow you back to earth if he could," Morgan remarked.

Morgan was sure the duty Mahihkan felt to protect Eli was why he'd agreed to Arik's suggestion to stay in Misewa, assuming he had the approval of the Chief and the Council. If the Great Bear Muskwa could change and become a part of the community, so could the wolf. Eli had told her once that Misewa meant "all that is" in the good words. But to Morgan, Misewa didn't just mean "all that is," it meant "all that could be."

Arik had offered to have Mahihkan stay at her longhouse, which excited Eli, because that's where he and Morgan stayed when they were on Askí. Although, if Emily started coming—and Morgan hoped she would—the longhouse would get too crowded. That was a problem they'd worry about another time, but it crossed Morgan's mind that a teepee might be a good solution. They'd stayed in a teepee when they'd journeyed to the past.

Arik and Emily were getting along famously, exchanging stories the whole way. Emily talked about hockey, and Arik followed along enthusiastically. Arik said the villagers of Misewa played a game just like it. They'd pass a ball made of deerskin stuffed with fur from one person to the other, catching it with mesh at the end of long, forked sticks. The object of the game was to throw the ball through two wooden posts that had been pounded into the ground.

"Oh, you mean lacrosse," Emily said.

"We just call it stick ball," Arik explained.

"You guys name things pretty literally over here, you know."

"What do you mean, 'literally'?"

"Like, things that move around under the ground: groundlings. Eli, a child, was stuck in a stone: Stone Child. You toss a ball from one stick to another: stick ball."

Mahihkan and Arik glanced at each other, wide-eyed, as though they'd been handed a revelation, but then shrugged simultaneously, accepting what was true and not apologizing for it.

"Would you prefer we call those creatures airlings?" Mahihkan asked.

"I did not just hear you make a joke," Emily teased.

"Don't hold your breath waiting to hear another one," the wolf said.

"Stick ball makes more sense than lacrosse," Arik said. "How does a word like that even relate to a game with a ball and sticks?"

"I wasn't saying it was a bad thing," Emily said.

Arik matched Emily's hockey stories with tales of the North Country, and Emily was enthralled by every word. These weren't just the stories that involved Morgan and Eli, but the legends of the Elders, tales that told the history of Misewa, and taught the community's values and ways of living.

Morgan and Eli seemed content to be with each other, and walked as quietly as Mahihkan, until Eli stated, "You left without me the night Mistapew took my soul. You said we'd never do that to each other."

Morgan nodded, admitting that her brother was right. "I know. I'm sorry. And if I hadn't done that, none of this would've happened."

"No," he said. "I was the one that followed you. If I hadn't followed you, and you'd slept at the Great Tree by yourself . . ."

"Then he would've taken my soul."

Morgan imagined how things might have changed, had the roles been reversed. When would Eli have found her?

"I should've just, like, gone to bed. On earth."

"But at least Emily got to see the North Country," Eli reasoned, "on the bright side of things."

"About that," Morgan said. "Speaking of things we said we'd never do. Like, bringing other people with us through

141

the portal. I needed her." What would she have done without Emily, who'd had so many good ideas during their quest? She couldn't even imagine. "I hope you're not mad about that. Or that you won't be once, you know, you've gotten over almost being dead."

Eli dismissed the notion with a wave of his hand, as if he were shooing away an insect. "I trust you, and if you trust her . . ."

And that was all he had to say.

"Emily loves it here," Morgan said, "and I love that she came, but still . . . I could've brought her another time and *not* put her in danger. Because I did. I put her in danger, and I put you in danger. All because . . ."

"All because what?" Eli asked. "Why'd you go through the portal without me?"

"I don't know, I . . ."

Morgan worked to stay calm. This journey had been good for one thing, at least: distracting her from the loss of her mother. At least up until the dream she'd had last night. It was as though Eli's safety was an invitation for the grief to return. She could feel it bubbling in her chest, pushing to get out.

"When I came into your bedroom that night and asked you if you were ready to go, you told me that you were too tired," Eli said.

"I know," Morgan said. "I was there."

"I wasn't finished," Eli said. "You told me that you were too tired, but you were crying. Something was wrong."

"You know me," Morgan said. "I get emotional. I was emotional. There doesn't have to be a reason."

She had never stopped to consider how she must have looked, lying there on her bed, crying. She'd thought he hadn't noticed.

"You're lying," Eli said, his tone pleading for her to tell him the truth.

Morgan did her best to stifle tears, but that bubbling grief was starting to boil. "I'm sorry I broke our promise. I could've cried anywhere. I could've cried right there in my bed. I just . . ." Morgan wiped tears away and bit her quivering lip. "I was mad and upset and I didn't want to be on earth. You and I are lucky—we have the option of going to another dimension if we don't want to be in this one. You know, because of climate change, or, like, a world war, or even . . ." Morgan breathed out steadily through her mouth, another attempt to suppress tears. "Even . . ."

"Morgan," Eli said gently. "Why were you mad and upset? You can tell me."

"I called my mother that night. Like, my birth mother. Katie got the number somehow. My kókom answered, and—"

"Your kókom!" Eli beamed. "That's amazing."

"Yeah, that's what I thought, too," Morgan said, "until I asked to speak to my mom. Jenny Trout, that's her name. That . . . was her name. My kókom told me that she died. I don't know when, I don't know how. But she's gone. She always was gone for me, and now she always will be gone. All I've got is that dream I told you about. That's all I'll ever have."

Eli stopped, which made Morgan stop, and he hugged her. At some point, Mahihkan must have looked back and noticed Morgan and Eli weren't with them anymore, that something was wrong, and so, a little distance ahead, the others stopped, too. And there they waited patiently, because, through the dead trees, the Barren Grounds were visible, along with the strong, broad trunk of the Great Tree.

"Those pictures on the Council Hut's walls," Eli said, "are memories. They're memories that live on in the people that keep them. They pass those memories down so that they never fade away. And the people in those memories are kind of immortal because of it."

"Kind of immortal isn't good enough. Kind of immortal doesn't bring my mom back to life. Stories don't bring my mom back to life. And somebody else's memories will never be my memories. I have one memory, Eli. *One*. I'll only ever have one."

Morgan held Eli harder.

"But Morgan," Eli said, "your kókom will have a whole lifetime to share with you. The things your mom did. What your mom was like. Don't you think that the stories Arik was telling Emily about Misewa made Misewa seem a bit more alive to her? Even though she's never been there before?"

"I don't know," Morgan said. "Maybe."

"You're right, your mother's gone . . . but you can still get to know her. Does that make sense?"

Did it? Morgan didn't know. She knew nothing about her mother, but if her kókom would see her, if her community would accept her just as Misewa had, she might learn something about Jenny Trout. Did Morgan look like her mother? Did she talk like her? Did she walk like her? Did she have the same mannerisms? Did she have the same smile? Would any of that make her mother seem alive? Morgan didn't have an answer. She didn't know if she believed that. It hurt too much right now for her to believe that.

"I've only known my mother in a dream," Morgan said. "And even if I get to know her through my kókom, she'll still never know me. She'll never know who I am. She'll never know that I didn't forget who I am. She'll never know . . . I forgive her. And that I'm okay."

"Are you . . . okay?" Eli asked.

"I thought I was," Morgan said. "Now I don't know."

TWENTY

Near midday, they emerged from the northern woods near the Great Tree and said their farewells. Arik promised to show Emily the whole southern woods when she returned, and Mahihkan promised Eli that he would be in Misewa waiting for him. Eli looked at once happy to be alive but downcast that he had to leave so soon after learning about Mahihkan's survival. More downcast than normal when it was time to leave the North Country.

Morgan stood off to the side on her own, lost in thought. Now that Eli was okay, there was nothing else to occupy her mind but Jenny Trout. Morgan didn't want to leave. She was already thinking of tomorrow, when she could come back. She could be away from earth, and hopefully the pain. She and Eli could bring Emily, and the three of them could go on more adventures. She could distract herself. Eight months in Misewa was enough time to get over a loss like the one she'd experienced, wasn't it?

"Morgan," Eli said. "Morgan."

He waved his hand in front of her face.

"Huh?"

"I said that we're ready to go."

"Oh," she said, "right. Okay."

The three children stepped up to the trunk of the Great Tree and discovered that Morgan had forgotten to close off the portal. It seemed untouched, though—nobody in or out—so no harm, no foul. How lucky they were that neither Katie nor James had woken early and gone upstairs to look for the siblings.

Emily was helping Morgan through the portal when they both noticed Eli staring at the tree, his hands pressed flat against the bark. Morgan, who'd begun to lower herself inside the attic, climbed back out and looked curiously at Eli. There didn't seem to be anything else in the North Country to him but the Great Tree, and he looked greatly concerned with it. She then did to her brother what he'd done to her on many occasions—she waved her hand in front of his face. She would have reveled in her revenge under different circumstances, but right now she was too curious.

"Eli," she said. "What're you doing?"

"Shhh," Eli said.

Morgan became so captivated with what Eli was doing that she wasn't even annoyed with him for shushing her. He was running his hands across the bark with his eyes closed, as though trying to communicate with it, interpreting whatever information the Great Tree was giving him. Then he pressed his ear against the trunk and listened. Morgan concentrated but she couldn't hear a thing. She noticed that everybody was watching Eli now.

"Eli," she said. "It's time to go."

"There's something in here," Eli said. "It's stuck inside. It wants to get out."

"It's stuck inside . . . the tree?"

"Oh!" Arik said excitedly. "Is it a squirrel? One time I was sleeping in a tree and there was this storm and *another* tree fell in front of the burrow I'd found, and it took me days to get out of there. It was terrifying."

"I think we'd be able to hear that kind of trapped thing," Emily said.

"That's true," Arik said. "I sounded like a four-legged squirrel, just chirping away like anything."

Mahihkan walked over to Eli and put his paw on the boy's shoulder. "What do you hear?"

Eli lifted his head from the bark, took his hands off the Great Tree, and scanned the group. "What did it feel like, when I was in the stone? Did you hear anything? Was anything different about it?"

Morgan shrugged. She'd carried it most of the time. "It didn't say anything to me, that's for sure."

"It just kind of glowed white," Emily said. "Like a night-light."

Morgan thought that was accurate. It was a light like the one she used to keep behind her headboard, for when the dark frightened her.

"It was a pretty stone, though," Arik said, "as stones go."

Eli backed away, and kept backing up until he had a full view of the Great Tree. Then he scanned all the trees that lined the northern woods, from west to east.

"I know that the trees deeper in the woods are all dead at the bottom because of the groundlings," he said. "But even at the tree line, they're . . . off. Like, the colors are muted. Do you see it?"

Morgan, along with the others, looked carefully, and Eli was right. The trees that were full, that hadn't yet lost their leaves close to the ground, still looked drained of life. She backed away until she stood beside Eli, and then gave the Great Tree the same attention. It was teeming with life in this autumn season, bright with reds, yellows, and oranges.

Each leaf was like a tiny flame.

"Why's it like that?" Morgan asked. "I don't get it."

"What gives us life? Humans, animals, all living things," he said.

Before, four days ago, Morgan might have said something more obvious. A beating heart. Blood. A brain. Lungs. Breathing in and out. But now, she knew more. Now, she knew better.

"A soul," she said.

"Exactly," he said.

"Wait a sec. You're saying . . ." Morgan gave the Great Tree a once-over. "You're saying there's a soul in the Great Tree?"

"*My* soul was in a rock, wasn't it?"

"Good point," Morgan conceded. "But whose soul?"

"Kihiw's," Eli said. "Kihiw's soul is in the Great Tree. It's been there since Mistapew took it."

"Mistapew put it in there?"

"Yes. He must have. Maybe that's why it's become a portal, because Kihiw's soul is in it." He paused, as though he didn't want to say what he said next. "That's why we have to release it."

"But how're we going to . . ." Morgan remembered the drawing outside the mouth of Mistapew's cave. There were animal beings and hunters by the Great Tree. The tree was on fire, and soaring above it was an eagle, its face pointing towards the sky. "I released your soul by heating the rock and creating steam," she said slowly. "We'll release Kihiw's soul by burning down the Great Tree?"

"Yes," Eli said. "Then he'll finally be free."

"Let me get this straight," Emily said, approaching Morgan, Eli, and Mahihkan with Arik. "You felt Kihiw's soul inside that tree?"

Eli nodded. "I felt it in my hands, then it ran through my body like blood."

"That's like being Force-sensitive," Emily said. "That's *so* cool."

"But children," Arik said, "if we burn down the Great Tree, we burn down the portal with it."

"I know," Morgan said. "But we couldn't leave Eli in the moon stone, and we can't leave Kihiw in that tree. If we can save him, we have to."

"Nicky said there were other portals in the North Country," Eli said. Nicky was Nikamon, Ochek's mother. Eli and Morgan had met her when they traveled to the past, to a time when Ochek was a teenager. "That means there are other ways to come back."

"She was right," Mahihkan said. "There are other portals. I've seen them."

"Yes, but one portal is tied to another." Arik was becoming frantic. "If you burn down this portal, the one in your attic won't work anymore."

"Arik, the children are right," the wolf said.

"You just found each other, Mahihkan, you and the boy," Arik said. "Now you're ready to never see him again?"

"If I know he'll be okay," the wolf said, "yes."

"We'll find another portal," Morgan said. "We found this one, and we weren't even looking. We'll find one that leads us back here, back to you guys." Morgan considered the possibility of being trapped on earth, never being able to return to Askí. To her relatives. To Misewa. She couldn't bear, or accept, the thought. And so she didn't. "We won't stop until we do."

Arik was crying, as though Eli were back in her arms and lifeless, as though there was more pain that required release. "Do you promise?" she asked.

Morgan lifted her up and held her tightly. "Of course I promise. You'll see us again. I can't imagine my life without this place. And níwakomakanak, my relatives."

"Because I'm not chopped liver, you know," Arik said.

They gathered wood from the tree line and built a bonfire near the Great Tree. This time, they didn't have to worry about summoning the groundlings, as Mahihkan reassured them that the creatures never strayed that far from their home. The fire was high enough, and bright enough, that many of the villagers soon joined them around the tree.

It was a peculiar gathering. Many of those who surrounded the Great Tree rejoiced, because Kihiw's tragic story had been told since time immemorial, from a time so long ago that nobody, not even the oldest among them, could remember when Mistapew had taken the eagle's soul. So long ago that some villagers didn't believe it was true at all. They considered it a story, a cautionary tale passed down through the generations and meant to scare villagers away from the northern woods. Morgan, too, had wondered whether the story of Kihiw was something like the old stories on earth that were made up to frighten children into good behavior: *Don't go near the northern woods or Mistapew might steal your soul!* She wondered no longer, though, because Eli's soul *had* been taken, and she'd come face to face with the giant.

Though there was great rejoicing, at the same time a pall of misery had been cast over the gathering. With the Great Tree gone, Morgan and Eli would have no way to return to Askí. Yes, there were other portals in the North Country, but where were the portals on earth that connected to them? How were the siblings going to find them?

While the fire raged, the animal beings and the humans said their goodbyes, and though Morgan uttered the same promise to each one of the villagers that she had to Arik, there nevertheless seemed to be an understanding that the siblings might never be seen again. There were many hugs, many tears, but time was running short, and the children couldn't postpone their departure any longer.

A handful of villagers took pieces of burning wood from the fire and stood ready to throw them high into the tree. At the very front of the crowd stood Arik, Mahihkan, Eli, Emily, Morgan, and, beside her, Muskwa. The Great Bear put his arm around Morgan and pressed her close against his fur before letting her go. He looked down at her and smiled with glistening, deep brown eyes.

"Silly old bear," Morgan said.

"I don't think I would be here if it weren't for you, Morgan," Muskwa said.

"Just be here when I get back, okay?"

Muskwa looked up to the sky, and so did Morgan. She knew that they were both imagining Ochek's constellation.

"As sure as the stars," he said. "How old do you think this silly old bear is?"

"More silly than old, I hope."

"You said once that anything could happen, and that I just needed to have faith in good people and good things."

"I remember that," Morgan said.

"Then I have faith we'll see each other again," Muskwa said.

Muskwa signaled for the torches to be thrown, and they flew through the air in streams of light to the Great Tree. They landed in the branches, and the crowd watched as the torches sparked small fires that cascaded over the entire tree with urgency, as though Kihiw himself was eager to escape a prison he'd been in for countless years. The heat started to become unbearable as the fire crawled closer to the ground, and the portal. There was an explosion at the very top. Seven trails of sparkling light shot into the sky, as though fireworks had been set off in celebration, then a plume of smoke rose from the flames and gradually took the shape of a massive eagle. The eagle, as if alive, let out a high-pitched whistle that sounded like a song, then flapped its wings and flew off towards the heavens before vanishing.

"Now, that's *B* for beautiful, Morgan," Emily said.

"Yeah," Morgan said. "Yeah, it is."

"Come, children!" Arik said, rushing towards the Great Tree.

Not only was the fire spreading towards the portal, the portal itself was collapsing into itself, vanishing before their very eyes. Kihiw's soul surely had given the tree magic, and now the magic was gone. The three humans ran for it. Emily climbed into the attic, followed by Eli. Morgan looked back at the villagers, her relatives, as the fire spread nearer to the hole that she and Eli had climbed through so many times before, a hole that was now only just big enough to allow her through.

"I'll be back," she said to them all.

Arik gave Morgan a paw and helped her through the portal, and Morgan held on until the portal was too small, and the heat too great.

"Kisakíhitin, dear one," Arik said.

"I love you, too, Arikwachas."

Then the portal closed like a tired eye, and inside the attic, the paper that had been affixed to the wall started to burn, having caught a spark from the Great Tree. Morgan, Eli, and Emily watched as the flame spread over the white parchment. It fell to the floor in embers. When those tiny sparks had died out, the three of them huddled in the middle of the secret room and held each other, until they heard rustling from the second floor.

Katie and James were awake.

TWENTY-ONE

Morgan listened to the sounds coming from the second floor to try to assess when they could leave the attic safely. That is, leave the attic without getting busted. She'd become very good at interpreting what her foster parents were doing simply by listening. For example, right now they were meandering around their bedroom, thinking about what to wear for the day, Katie perhaps combing her hair, James putting on his watch. Depending on when they'd gotten out of bed, this would take them five or ten minutes. After that, they'd leave their bedroom.

While Morgan was listening for her foster parents, Emily walked over to where the portal had been. She ran her hand over the slanted roof, testing the space the picture had covered.

"It's not even hot," she said. "That tree was burning like crazy."

"As soon as the portal's closed, Askí disappears," Morgan

explained. "It's wherever it is, whatever reality it's in . . . just, like, not here."

"There's just shingles and pigeon crap on the other side of that roof now," Eli said.

"That's literally true," Morgan said. "We went to the backyard and looked one day. There's a big pile of pigeon crap, and there's always a pigeon or two walking around up there."

"Just walking around," Emily said.

"And crapping, I guess," Morgan said.

"And now Askí is . . . gone? I mean, you won't be able to get back there from here, unless you find another portal?" Emily asked.

Morgan didn't want to think about that. Only three days ago, she'd had so many things—everything she could ever want. She had a foster home that wasn't awful—that was actually pretty great. She had a best friend, and maybe more, in Emily, somebody she trusted enough to share the most unbelievable secret with, somebody she could be completely vulnerable around. She had a brother, somebody she could rely on, and who, in turn, could rely on her. She had Misewa, another home, and a place that had helped her to understand who she was and to feel strong in her identity. And somewhere at the end of a phone line, she had a mother who had never wanted to lose Morgan, and who would finally have her back.

Now, this morning, she'd almost lost her brother, she had lost her mother, and until they figured out how to get back there, she'd lost Misewa, too.

Morgan ignored Emily's question.

"We'd better get to our bedrooms," Morgan said. "We can't get caught up here or . . ."

But then her heart sank.

"Or what?" Emily said.

"They won't let us hang out up here anymore," Eli said.

By the tone of his voice, sullen and deflated, Morgan knew that Eli understood what she did.

"It doesn't matter," Morgan said. "If we get caught up here, if they keep us from going to the attic, it doesn't make a difference. The portal won't open anymore. There's no reason to be here. When they finish the renovations I still won't come up here. The joke's on them if they ban us."

"I won't come up here either," Eli said. "It'll hurt too much."

"But you guys *are* going to find another portal, right?" Emily asked. "That's what Arik said to do."

"Where, Emily? Do you know of any, like, magical wardrobes lying around?" Morgan snapped. She covered her eyes, trying to keep her tears at bay. "I'm sorry. I just . . . I have no idea where to look. In another attic? Do we start breaking into random houses and, like, staple pictures onto their attic walls?"

Emily moved Morgan's hand away from her eyes. "You sounded so sure that you'd be back when we were on Askí," Emily said. "You said that you wouldn't give up until you found a portal."

"And I won't," Morgan said. "I'm just so scared that I'll never find one."

"Being scared has never stopped you before," Eli said.

"Yeah, I know." Morgan wiped at her cheeks to remove tears she hadn't been able to thwart. "Thanks for reminding me." She took a breath in . . . and let a breath out. "I guess we should go. It might not matter if we're banned from the attic, but it'll be hard to find another portal if we're grounded."

They left their secret room, probably for the last time, and crept down the two flights of stairs to the second floor. Morgan turned the doorknob slowly and pushed the door to the hallway open a crack. Katie and James's bedroom door was closed. For the moment, the coast was clear. Morgan opened the door all the way. Eli darted across the hall and into his bedroom. Morgan and Emily watched as he climbed into his bed fully clothed and covered himself in the Star Wars comforter.

"Our turn," Morgan whispered to Emily.

She leapt into the hallway with the agility of a teenager who'd snuck around the house more than once and took a sharp left turn towards her bedroom. Emily was right behind her, but as soon as Morgan made it into her room, James popped into the hallway like a jack-in-the-box. The girls didn't even bother moving another inch. He had seen at least one of them, and maybe both. Morgan was fully in her bedroom and Emily was frozen in the doorway, as though protecting herself from an earthquake.

"What's going on here?" James asked.

Neither of the girls turned around.

"Morgan, is that you?"

Morgan and Emily looked nothing alike. Morgan was tall, lean, and olive-skinned, with black hair. Emily was short and powerful, white, and had dirty-blond hair. But they were both wearing hooded sweatshirts, Morgan's bedroom light was off, the sun still hadn't risen, and the light from James's room wasn't that bright. More footsteps in the hallway—these were less explosive than James's. Katie had joined him.

"What are you doing up so early?" Katie asked. "You're never up until breakfast is ready."

"And then you almost never eat it," James added.

Morgan racked her brain for some way out of this. They'd made it out of the attic without being seen, but now, while she was out of sight, Emily was standing in her bedroom doorway in full view of her foster parents. And to make matters worse, Morgan and Emily were facing away from the hallway, not towards it, which meant they were coming *from* somewhere, not going *to* somewhere. At just after six o'clock in the morning. There weren't a lot of options. In fact, Morgan quickly realized that there were exactly zero options. Morgan motioned for Emily to turn around and reveal herself to Katie and James.

"I've got a bad feeling about this," Emily whispered to Morgan.

"It'll be fine," Morgan whispered back. "Just follow my lead. Honestly, they'll be so happy I have a friend they might not even get mad."

"A friend?" Emily said.

Morgan blushed. It was dark, but Emily must have seen it, because she smiled at Morgan's nonverbal response.

"Who are you talking to?" James asked.

Emily turned towards Katie and James with her hands up, as though it were a stickup.

Morgan walked past Emily and stepped into the hallway, lowering Emily's arms on the way while whispering, "They're not going to shoot you."

There they were, standing side by side outside Morgan's bedroom. Morgan was still blushing.

"I was talking to Emily." She pointed at Emily as though Emily were not the only other girl in the hallway. And then, for good measure, in case it wasn't crystal clear, she added, "This is Emily."

Emily waved at Katie and James. "Hey, I'm Emily. Good morning."

"Good morning," James said, sounding every bit as confused as he looked.

By this time, Eli had heard the commotion, got out of bed, and was hovering around his bedroom door, watching and listening.

"Hi, Emily," Katie said, unable to hide, as Morgan had predicted, how pleased she was that Morgan had a friend over. Forget that it was super early in the morning and they were fully clothed and had obviously been sneaking around. "It's nice to meet you."

"Where were you two just now?" James asked. "And, no offence," he added to Emily, "but what are you even doing here?"

He clearly was not as pleased as Katie, or not pleased enough to ignore the strangeness of the situation. Morgan couldn't blame him, but she had no idea what to say about it other than to blurt out, "Emily slept over."

That only solved half the problem—there was still the question of where they had been, which, judging by James's face alone, needed to be answered.

Thankfully, Emily was quick on her toes, adding, "We were in the attic watching the sun come up. It was very romantic. You guys should check it out one morning."

She must have noticed the big window in the main attic room that had been under construction for a billion years, and it just so happened to look east, where the sun rose. It made Morgan think of the sweat lodge. *If the sun didn't rise, there'd be no life.* No life. The train of thought led back to her mother.

Katie and James seemed to buy the story—she nodded, and he shrugged—but then Katie asked, "Just how late did Emily come over last night? When we were in bed, nobody was here. And you were in bed already."

It was a great point. Katie was asking some very parent-like questions. Day after day, she was developing mom intuition: the uncanny ability to sniff out a lie. Morgan was up to the challenge, and ready to lie convincingly to Katie, but only because there was truth to her emotions. She'd just thought of her mother, whom she'd been thinking of often since Eli had been saved. She liked that Katie was getting the hang of this whole mom thing, but at the same time, it almost felt like cheating on her birth mother. As though, if she accepted Katie as a mom, even as a foster mom, it made Jenny *less* her mother. Morgan hated using her sadness to convince Katie of something that wasn't true, but she didn't want her foster parents to not allow Emily over again. And she didn't want to be grounded.

"I called my mother last night, after I went to bed. It took me a long time to build up the courage. I didn't know when I was going to call," Morgan said, "but I just picked up my phone and did it."

If anybody wanted to say anything, something like, "And then what happened?" or "What did she say?" they didn't.

Morgan paused, trying to summon the words. She could feel them at the pit of her stomach. She hadn't even told Emily what happened. Just Eli. Eli, who had now left his bedroom and was standing beside her for moral support. For even more support, she reached out and found Emily's hand. She took it, and interlaced her fingers with Emily's. Emily must have known something was wrong. She held Morgan's hand firmly. A hockey grip. Morgan breathed in, and stuttered a breath out. She didn't even bother trying to stop the tears.

"My grandmother, my kókom, answered, and I was . . . so excited. I thought, 'I have a kókom, too?' You know, like, two weeks ago I never thought that I'd meet my mother, and now I was going to meet my grandmother?"

Morgan smiled, allowing herself a moment in time to imagine a different reality where her mother was alive. She allowed herself to imagine a life with her, and then, just like that, the vision was gone.

"I asked to speak with Jenny Trout." She glanced at Emily. "That's my mother's name. Jenny Trout. My kókom got weird, and told me . . ."

Morgan keeled over, sobbing. Emily held her up. Morgan could hardly catch her breath. When she'd told Eli, she'd not been able to let out all the emotions that had been welling up inside. She did now. But there in the hallway, with Emily holding her up, with her foster parents and Eli laying their hands on her shoulders, Morgan started to realize her tears weren't only for her mother. They were for being taken away so young. They were for losing her language. They were for losing her culture. They were for the homes she'd lived in. They were for the love she'd never received. And they were for having that love now, on earth and in Misewa. They were for all of these things—what had been taken and what had been found.

"She told me that my mother was dead."

There was no holding her up then. Emily eased Morgan down to the floor, and everybody huddled around her. Emily had Morgan's head on her lap, Eli had his hand on her arm, Katie and James were holding her hands. Morgan was just lying there. She knew the others were with her, but she was staring at the blank white ceiling.

It was so quiet, as though the world had turned off the sound. But then she heard footsteps crunching through snow, coming towards her through the white. She'd collapsed in the deep, untouched snow of the Barren Grounds. The footsteps came closer, and Morgan realized it was her heart beating.

Thump. Thump. Thump. Thump. Thump. Thump. Thump.

Ochek was in front of her, extending a paw towards her. She took it, and he helped her to her feet.

"You saved my life," she said.

"And you saved mine, Morgan," he said.

"What do I do now?" she asked.

"You keep trying to find your way," he said. "Every step is a part of that journey."

"Where? Back to Misewa?"

"No, back to you."

Ochek smiled at her, then turned away.

Morgan rubbed her eyes, and found that she was still in the hallway. Emily helped her to her feet. Everybody was staring at her. Ochek was gone, but what had Muskwa said to her once?

To live in the hearts of others is not to die.

Okay, she thought. *Okay, I get it. My mother's gone, but not really.*

Then, as though in affirmation, there was a low roar. The Great Bear? No. Morgan held her stomach. She'd not eaten since yesterday.

"You know what?" she said weakly.

"What?" Katie said.

"What do you need?" James said. "Anything we can do . . ."

Emily had her arm around Morgan, in case she might collapse again.

"I'm here," Emily said.

"We all are," Eli said.

"Ekosani." Morgan looked each of them in the eyes, ending with Emily. "Honestly, this might seem anticlimactic, but I think right now I could use some food."

"I can do that," Katie said. "I can make all the things you like."

"And I'll make some coffee," James said. "Black, right?"

Morgan nodded. That was exactly how she liked her coffee.

TWENTY-TWO

Katie wasn't kidding about making all the things Morgan liked; she may have made all the things, period. On the dining room table were serving dishes and bowls full of hash browns, scrambled eggs, bacon, sausages, sliced oranges, granola, yogurt, strawberries, blueberries, and toast, and a selection of spreads—margarine, peanut butter, jam, and marmalade—were laid out. There was also a jug of orange juice and a pot of coffee. On a normal morning, there was no way that five people could have finished all the food that Katie had prepared, but this was not a normal morning. In the North Country, Eli had eaten a sizable helping of pimíhkán, but still, he hadn't eaten anything in the three days prior. And Morgan and Emily hadn't eaten since yesterday. Within seconds of Katie welcoming the kids to dig in, their plates were full, and so were their mouths.

"This is so good I could eat ten helpings," Emily said. "Can I eat here all the time?"

"I really appreciate you being here for Morgan," Katie replied, "but maybe from now on the sleepovers shouldn't be on school nights."

"Katie's right," James said. "You guys already got yourselves overtired this week, remember? It made you sick."

"I think we were probably getting sick anyway," said Eli, who was eating as much as the girls. "That's why."

"Still, I think that's fair," Katie said. "Today is Friday. Emily's welcome to stay over tonight if she wants."

Morgan looked at Emily hopefully. "Do you want to? It might be nice to have some company. We could watch *Empire Strikes Back*. Make popcorn . . ." She leaned towards Emily, waiting for a response, but when she didn't get one right away, she said, "I mean, we just spent the night together. You're probably all Morgan-ed out. I get it."

"Relax, Morg. My mouth was full," Emily said. "But maybe *you're* all Emily-ed out?"

"No," Morgan said quickly. "Not at all."

"Okay, so, throw in *Rogue One* and I'm sold."

"We can throw in *Rogue One* and the *entire* original trilogy."

"Oh *ho*!" Emily laughed. "You don't mess around, do you?"

"Not when it comes to Star Wars."

Eli was eating even more now, trying not to show how left out he felt, but failing. Morgan noticed.

"How about it, bro?" Morgan said. "You up for a Star Wars marathon? I think you have to earn that comforter before I steal it from you."

Eli beamed. "I've been wanting to see what Hoth looks like," he said.

"Trust me," Morgan said, "you've seen what Hoth looks like."

The kids laughed. The adults looked confused, but they shrugged it off, happy as they were to see the kids behaving like kids. Eating like kids, talking like kids, planning kid things. The levity was what likely emboldened Katie to circle back to the subject of Morgan's family. But she seemed very careful not to mention Jenny Trout.

"So, do you think you'll get back in touch with your kókom?" Katie asked, dabbing at her bottom lip, where some stray morsels of scrambled eggs had rested. "When you think you're ready, that is."

"I don't know." Morgan started to poke at her food rather than eat it. "Maybe. Probably. She's like family, right?"

"She's not *like* family, she *is* family," Katie said.

"Níwakomakanak," Morgan whispered.

"What was that?" James asked. "Cree? What does it mean?"

Morgan pointed a fork at her brother. "Eli's been teaching me some words. That means 'my relatives.'"

"That's wonderful," Katie said. "That's just wonderful."

"Very cool," James said. "That's important. You know, getting in touch with—"

Morgan shot James a look, in a very Katie-like move. "James, don't." Then, very Morgan-like, she recognized that she was close to a blowup and took a breath. "Please."

Katie nudged James, elbow to hip, and shook her head.

James cleared his throat.

"It's great," he said. "It's really great."

"Thanks," Morgan said.

She blindly scooped a forkful off her plate, a sampling of pretty much everything on it, and shoved it all in her mouth. She chewed it methodically, then swallowed. She took another sip of coffee, then pulled the Post-it Note out of her pocket, where it had found a home since Katie had given it to her. She tossed it onto the table. It had become more crumpled than folded, and it opened on its own like a blossoming flower, revealing a few digits of the phone number in the process.

"The number's right here if I want to use it, right? It's programmed into my phone, too. In fact, who needs this?"

Morgan tossed it away without aiming. It landed in Eli's bacon.

"Thanks?" he said. He picked the paper out of his bacon with his thumb and index finger.

"Sorry!" Morgan executed a dramatic double facepalm.

"It's fine," he said. "There's lots of meat to go around."

"Not for long," Emily said, scooping more bacon onto her plate.

"You should keep this, though," Eli said to Morgan, "in case something weird happens to your phone."

"Eli's got a point," James said. "Sometimes my phone craps out and I lose everything."

"That's because you're, like, almost forty," Morgan said, and realized immediately that she'd been rude. "Sorry. *Again.* I'm just going to preemptively apologize to everybody because I'm obviously going to snap at all of you at some point over breakfast."

"You get a pass this morning," James said. "But really, keep it. You never know."

"I don't have to keep it, I've already memorized the stupid number," Morgan said, and then to prove it she recited all ten digits.

"Wait," Eli said. "That's it? For real?"

"*Yeah*," Morgan said impatiently, "why would I make a phone number up?"

"That's a Norway House number," Eli said.

"How would you even know that?" Morgan asked.

"Because I'm from Cross Lake. My reserve and your reserve are neighbors."

"What? Shut up."

"I'm serious," Eli said. "We used to take a boat to visit. There's a bunch of little waterfalls along the river, and there are trees everywhere you look. And wildlife. Beavers, muskrats, eagles. We used to visit there, and when I go . . . when I *went* . . . out on the land with my grandpa, his trapline's between the two reserves."

"Well." Morgan composed herself. "Who knew? Neighbors. Maybe that's why we get along so well, bro."

"Maybe you guys are cousins!" Emily said. "Sorry if that's ignorant. Actually, that's for sure ignorant."

"No, it's not." Eli chuckled. "Some stereotypes are kind of true. I've got tons of cousins in both communities."

"What would be the chances of that?" James mused. "Randomly placed into the same house and ending up being family. It's like right out of a book."

"It certainly wasn't planned," Katie added.

"They probably would've let you know," Morgan said.

"Well, they didn't let me know about . . ." Katie started, then stopped.

Morgan knew what she was going to say, though, and Katie was about to make a good point. Nobody had told Katie or James about her mother being dead. It was unbelievable that they hadn't, but no less true. If they weren't going to provide that information, why would they tell her foster parents that Eli was a relative?

"It doesn't make a difference." Morgan locked eyes with Eli. "You are family, either way. You always will be, and nothing can make it different."

"I think it's awesome how close you two have become in two weeks," James said. "We were so worried at first, right, Katie?"

"It just goes to show you that worry never solves a thing," Katie said.

Everybody at the table started eating again. Morgan wasn't sure what Emily and Eli were thinking, but the morning had—incredibly, against all odds—turned around. Though Katie thought she messed up all the time, she actually did a lot of things well, because, as Eli would say, she did them with a good heart. Something as simple as making breakfast. Morgan had learned, from her time in Misewa, that food was medicine. She knew that being with family was, too. Yes, she'd lost her mother, but somewhere up north she had a grandmother. Even closer, she had all the people surrounding her at the dining room table, and it gave her hope that something else incredible could happen. That she could find the relatives she'd left behind in another reality.

Now *that*, Morgan thought, would be like something right out of a book.

TWENTY-THREE

Katie and James told Eli and Morgan that, all things considered, they could take the day off school. But they opted to go anyway. If the portal hadn't been closed permanently, that might have changed things. But the portal *had* been closed, and staying home would have been too upsetting.

The three friends walked quickly, because they were in danger of being late thanks to their breakfast feast. Morgan and Eli knew that Katie would handle any issues with the school, but Emily's parents thought she'd gone to school early to work out in the gym, and being late would land her in trouble. Her parents were strict. If she didn't get good grades, or if she missed class without a legitimate reason, they would keep her home from hockey.

"They'd do that? Just for being late once?" Morgan asked. "Holy."

"One late isn't *that* big a deal," Emily said, "but we already skipped class this week."

Morgan apologized for what felt like the hundredth time that morning, but Emily wouldn't have any of it. She told Morgan she was a big girl and could make her own decisions. *She* had suggested they skip class, and *she* had agreed to come over early, and *she* was glad for it.

"If I miss a hockey practice, *come on*," she said. "I went to another world with you."

Still, the siblings felt the least they could do for such a good friend was get to school on time. All the way there, they talked of their adventure. Emily was still trying to make sense of it, and Eli had been asleep for most of it.

"And dude, it's so crazy that I came to your house this morning," Emily said, "but we spent *four days* in the northern woods! *What?*"

"The time thing is pretty crazy," Morgan said. "I'm still not even sure how it works. Like, time moves faster there, right? One week there is an hour here. But I don't think people age faster. Actually, I think they age really slowly."

"Arik doesn't know how old she is," Eli added, "but she must be hundreds of years old."

"That explains why you guys have been there for two years and, Morgan, you're still thirteen," Emily said. "I mean, you look thirteen, anyway."

"That must be how it works, because I'm *for sure* still twelve," Eli said, then raised a flat hand over his head to show that he was still short.

"Your foster dad said he couldn't believe how close you guys have gotten in two weeks." Emily laughed. "Which is hilarious, because, thanks to being in Misewa, you guys have known each other for ages."

"That *is* funny," Morgan said. "Just wait until you come with us. In a month you'll have known me for years, too."

"Yeah," Emily said, "we'll be like *The Golden Girls.*"

They didn't speak much after that, and Morgan knew why. Though she remained hopeful that one day they'd find their way back to Askí, to their family in Misewa, nobody had any idea how. It was just that: hope. Hope didn't offer answers, and that's what they needed if they were ever to return.

They got to school before the bell rang and went straight to class, but it was impossible for Morgan to concentrate. Emily had recently told her that she seemed distant all the time. Morgan hadn't realized it was obvious to others, but it was true. No matter what class Morgan was in, she paid little attention, and her grades had suffered as a result. The B+ Mrs. Edwards had given her two weeks ago for the poem she'd rewritten was the peak of her academic performance recently; she'd gotten a C on another assignment for writing about an encounter she and Arik had had with a skittish porcupine, how they'd almost been impaled by her quills.

"This was supposed to be a journal entry," Mrs. Edwards wrote on the paper in bold red ink, "not fantasy."

And Morgan didn't even want to think about her Math mark. The only math she cared about was Misewa Math. Instead of putting effort into writing a short story, or solving an equation, Morgan was typically daydreaming, passing the time, waiting for night to arrive so she could go to Misewa with Eli.

Now Morgan *and* Emily were distracted. The difference was that they weren't writing stories about the adventure they'd just had. They weren't struggling over an algebra problem. They weren't daydreaming. They were brainstorming how they could get back to Askí. They spent both of their morning classes sitting awkwardly upright and using their phones under their desks, out of sight.

In English class, they texted each other ideas about where a portal might be.

Morg: What about that forest off Grant Avenue?
Houldsy: Assiniboine Forest?
Morg: Yeah
Houldsy: That's not actually a forest it's a walking trail
Morg: SMH
Houldsy: What about somewhere in Whiteshell Park?
That's an actual forest
Morg: So we're just going to walk all around the Whiteshell?
That'll take years
Houldsy: We need specifics
Morg: Bigfoot sightings!
Houldsy: Genius

Morgan reasoned that when people on earth saw a bigfoot, it *had* to be the same creature that was known on Askí as Mistepew. What were the odds that these were completely different big hairy monsters? So that meant the bigfoots were using a portal between the two worlds, in the same way she and Eli and Emily did.

Find a bigfoot . . . find a portal!

The googling of bigfoot sightings took place during Math class. When the teacher saw Morgan on her phone, she switched to her calculator app and showed him random numbers she'd quickly punched in.

"Just confirming an answer," she said innocently, and he fell for it, or didn't care. Whatever the reason, he didn't take her phone away.

They did a deep dive into bigfoot research that started with the classic Patterson-Gimlin film from 1967. The film clearly shows the female bigfoot that humans called Patty. Patty, a hairy bipedal figure, walks across a clearing, over what looks to be a surface as gray as the northern woods, towards the forest. At one point, she looks over her shoulder, right at the camera. Morgan thought the creature looked a lot like Mistapew, only shorter. She read that Patty was maybe seven feet tall. The giant they'd encountered was at least ten feet.

Morgan excitedly sent the video to Emily.

Morg: Check this out!
Houldsy: Seen it! That's like the first thing that comes up when you google bigfoot sightings

The film didn't help much anyway. Whether it was real (Morgan thought it was) or a hoax, the video was shot near a place called Orleans, California. That was almost

1,400 miles from Winnipeg, according to Google Maps. There was no way they were going that far to search the woods for a portal. Katie and James wanted to make Morgan happy, but she very much doubted that would stretch as far as a trip to California.

The videos they found were increasingly absurd. In one, somebody was clearly wearing a modified Chewbacca suit. In another, the bigfoot was so far away it looked like a speck. There was one that had been taken in the winter on a mountain in British Columbia, looking down into a valley. The figure was easy to spot, dark brown against white snow, but could have been anything, like a hiker wearing a puffy black snowsuit. But then it hit her. Eli had mentioned a film somebody had taken of a bigfoot between Norway House and Fisher River. By Eli's own admission it had probably just been a bear, but what if it wasn't? Even if there was the smallest chance, it had to be worth a shot.

Morg: I think I have a plan
Houldsy: Find something?
Morg: Maybe
Houldsy: I just started watching Star Wars videos TBH. Gave up
Morg: Chewbacca, right?
Houldsy: Yeah
Morg: I found something IRL
Houldsy: Tell me!

Morgan looked at the clock. Class would be over in a few minutes. She typed one word back to Emily.

Morg: Lunch.

Eli was already in the lunchroom when Morgan and Emily rushed inside. They found him sitting on the floor by himself in the corner, drawing, which is what he always did when the girls couldn't convince him to sit with them. By the looks of it, *his* research had consisted of drawing Mistapew as the creature had been described to him. Considering that he'd not actually seen the giant with his own eyes, the likeness was remarkable. Morgan was impressed, as she usually was by his artwork. His sketch looked more accurate than any of the bigfoot videos she'd watched in Math class.

He was so into his work that he didn't notice the girls at first. Morgan had to nudge his arm with her foot. He made an errant stroke with his pencil.

"Hey!" He busily erased the mistake.

"Come sit with us," Morgan said.

"Can I just finish this?" he asked.

"Nope."

"That's rude. I'm in the middle of something."

"Dude, Morg's got a plan," Emily said. "She's really excited about it, and I don't think she's going to leave you alone until you come sit with us. You know how stubborn she is."

Eli closed the drawing pad and got to his feet. "Yes, I do know how stubborn she is."

"I'm literally standing right here, you know," Morgan said.

"Yeah," Eli said, "and *you* know how stubborn you are, too."

"That's fair," she said.

They found an empty spot at the end of one of the long lunch tables, far enough away from other students that nobody would overhear their conversation. There, they huddled together as though they were a gossipy clique, and Morgan began to lay out her scheme.

"First, let me just say that I know this is totally dependent on whether or not the bigfoot sighting I'm talking about is legit," Morgan said. "If it's not, we're back to square one."

"What bigfoot sighting?" Eli asked.

"The one you told me about before," Morgan said. "The one, I should add, that I found on the internet today and watched!" Her voice had escalated during that last sentence, until it was loud enough for others to hear. She corrected herself, paraphrasing what she'd just said, only now in a whisper. "I found it on YouTube and watched it."

"I'm not even sure that video isn't a prank," Eli said.

"The guy who shot it seemed sincere in the interview," Morgan said defensively. "I believed him, anyway."

"What?" Eli said. "The interview on TMZ?"

"TMZ's usually accurate, you know," Morgan said.

"Morg, I want to go back to Askí and see everything you've told me about," Emily said, "but . . . do you think it's possible that, maybe, you just *want* to believe him?"

"There are thousands of bigfoot-sighting videos," Eli added.

"So, wait," Morgan said. "He took your soul, chased us through the northern woods, we killed him, and you're suggesting that he's a hoax?"

"That's not what I'm saying," Eli said. "I believed Mistapew was real before all that happened. I'm saying that a lot of people make up these sightings and fake their videos for attention, to get famous for a few seconds."

"Would people from your community make it up to get famous if Mistapew is something they believe in?" Morgan asked.

"I don't know, maybe," Eli said. "It's not like just because we're Cree we're all saints. We can do bad things like anybody else. You can believe in something and still want to get attention on social media—it doesn't mean that thing you believe in isn't real."

"Oh my god, Eli, a simple 'yes' would've been fine. I didn't ask you to philosophize, or whatever that was," Morgan snapped, and she caught herself raising her voice for a second time. She lowered it. "We need to focus. Did anybody else have any bright ideas?"

"I didn't," Emily said.

"I didn't either," Eli said. "I just gave up and started drawing."

"As one does," Morgan said. "Anyway, that video was good, as bigfoot videos go. It was grainy and everything but, like, I don't think it was a bear. It was pretty tall for a bear. And it was walking."

Emily turned to Eli. "Before we rush to judgment, we should hear what her plan actually is. Your sister's pretty smart."

"I know," Eli said. "I'm sorry, Morgan. I just don't want to get my hopes up."

"I'd rather be disappointed than never try, wouldn't you?" Morgan asked, but when Eli didn't answer, she just continued. "Okay, first off, you know where the sighting was, right? You said around your grandfather's trapline?"

"Right," Eli said. "Like, between our two communities, just off the river."

"Perfect," Morgan said. "That's what I thought."

"You want to go there, don't you?" Emily asked.

Morgan nodded her head animatedly. "All three of us. We could, like, spend the whole weekend looking for it. If we find it, we could spend a few weeks in Misewa maybe. If we don't . . ." Morgan threw up her hands. "Oh well, we gave it a shot."

"We can't just . . . go to Norway House," Eli said. "Katie and James would have to drive us. I'm twelve, you guys are thirteen. We don't have licenses."

"Oh, they'll drive us," Morgan said. Then she looked at Emily. "Do you think your parents would let you go?"

"Probably, if there are adults taking us," Emily said. "I don't have hockey this weekend. But, Morg—"

"Do you think Katie and James are going to take us to Norway House to look for bigfoot?" Eli asked, finishing Emily's sentence.

Morgan was undeterred.

"I don't think they're going to drive us to look for big-foot," she said. "But they bought me moccasins. They brought me a First Nations feast. They tracked down my mother's name and number. I never even had to ask. So, if I ask to see my kókom in Norway House . . ."

"They'll take us," Eli said.

"In a heartbeat," Morgan said.

"That could work."

"Are you . . ." Emily's tone softened. She reached out and put her hand on top of Morgan's. "Are you going to be okay, seeing your kókom? If we go to see her, you'll have to *actually* see her. We can wait, if it's too soon, or too hard."

Morgan flipped her hand over and clasped Emily's hand, as though anticipating the support she knew she'd need for a visit like that.

"I . . . I want to meet her, and I want to know more about my mom. I didn't think it would be so soon but, like, however long we wait, Misewa will be waiting even longer for *us*. I'll be okay."

"Alright. I'm in," Emily said. "Of course I am."

"Me too," Eli said. "Let's do it."

TWENTY-FOUR

During the last class of the day, Morgan excused herself to go to the bathroom, and she locked herself in a stall. She knew there was a decent chance she'd get some privacy there—in fact, that's where she'd gone earlier in the week when she and Emily had skipped class to talk. They'd ducked into a stall when they heard someone coming, and that someone had turned out to be Eli, hiding from the bullies who had been targeting him.

Thinking about it now, Morgan realized that those bullies were noticeably quiet today. It was only yesterday that pretty much the entire school had stood up to them in support of Eli and Morgan. In fact, Morgan wasn't sure if the bullies were at school at all.

"They're probably somewhere looking for their pride," she whispered to herself as she sat on the toilet lid, curling her knees up to her chest.

She'd been thinking about them to gather courage, to remind herself that she could do hard things. She could stand up to bullies. She could stand up to a violent, greedy man aiming an arrow at her head. She could stand up to a Great Bear. She could stand up to a giant. All of these things somehow seemed as easy as breathing right now. There she was, holding her phone, her kókom's number locked and loaded, and all she had to do was press that thumb-sized green button with the white phone icon. But her thumb, hovering just over the glass surface, couldn't quite finish the job. She was watching her thumb as though it might move on its own, as though it might summon the bravery she was trying to muster, and wondering why it was so hard. She'd called her before. She'd called her last night.

"Yeah, and it was the worst phone call in the history of the world," she said, once more answering her thoughts.

But there was no other way to get to Norway House, to try to find the portal, to get to know her mother outside of a dream. She took a deep breath in, a long breath out, and then closed her eyes and lowered her thumb until she felt the cool glass surface. With one eye open, she looked down at the device, and saw that her aim had been true, like a round stone from a slingshot. Before she could think about hanging up, Morgan raised the phone to her ear.

"Tansi?" an older woman's voice answered.

Her kókom.

Morgan cleared her throat. She forced out a greeting, because if she waited too long, her kókom might hang up, and she was worried she wouldn't find the courage to call again.

"Tansi," she said.

"Who's this?" her kókom asked.

"Hi," Morgan said, as though she hadn't just said hi in Cree. "Hi," she said again, nervously, then admitted, "I don't really know what to say."

"You sound like the girl who called last night," her kókom said.

"I . . . I am," Morgan said. "That was me. I'm so sorry for hanging up. I was just . . . I didn't . . ."

"It's okay, my girl," her kókom said. "It's okay."

Morgan tried to calm herself again, but when she spoke, her voice was still shaky. "I called to talk to my . . . to Jenny . . . and I didn't expect that she . . . that she . . ." Morgan cupped her hand to her mouth and closed her eyes, blinking out tears. She couldn't stop the tears, didn't want to stop the tears, but didn't want her kókom to hear her whimpering over the phone.

"She died earlier this year," her kókom said, sounding as though she, too, was trying to keep her voice steady. "She died not that long ago."

"How . . ." Morgan moved some hair behind her ear, sniffled, took another breath. She started to fidget with her moccasins, brushing her fingertip back and forth over the soft fur. "How did she die?"

"Who is this?" her kókom asked again, in a kind way.

"It's Morgan. I'm Morgan Trout. I'm—"

"Nósisim?" her kókom said.

Morgan felt breathless. "Kókom."

"My girl. My grandchild. Is it really you?"

"It's really me," Morgan said, and she broke into a wide smile. Saying her name, telling her kókom who she was, felt healing. "It's really me."

"Your mother and I dreamed that one day we'd be with you again," her kókom said.

"You mean . . ." Morgan felt her salty tears slide across her upturned lips. "I mean, she didn't . . . she didn't let me go?"

"No," her kókom said urgently, "oh no, my girl. She would never have let you go. You were taken from her."

Morgan felt some of the heaviness lift from her chest. Somewhere deep down she'd known it, but hearing it meant everything.

"I dreamed of her, too," Morgan said. "And I dreamed that, I don't know, that I wouldn't have to dream about her anymore."

"I know, my girl," her kókom said. "I'm sorry. But you'll get to know her more from me, and maybe I'll get to know more about her, from you." She paused for a few seconds. "Maybe we both won't miss her as much."

Morgan was running her fingers over the tiny beads on her footwear, as though she were reading Braille, as though a story were written in the white, snowflake-like design. And maybe there was, but not the kind of story she wanted to hear.

"How did she die?" Morgan asked again.

"Oh, nósisim," her kókom said. Then she paused again, this time for longer than a few seconds. When she spoke at last, it was quietly, and carefully. "She died of loneliness. I think that's the best way to tell you. She died of loneliness."

"That doesn't tell me much," Morgan said, matching the volume of her kókom's voice, still tracing the beadwork with her finger.

"I think," her kókom said, "that one day you'll be able to know more. But for right now, nósisim, maybe that's enough."

Morgan nodded, as though her kókom could see her. She understood. They'd only just met, had only just been on the phone for a few minutes. There were some things that shouldn't be said over the phone. There were some things that needed to be said in person.

"Do you think I could come there?" Morgan asked.

"My girl," her kókom said, "of course you can come here. You can come here anytime. You are always welcome here. It's your home."

"How about tomorrow?" Morgan asked hopefully. "Would I be welcome there tomorrow? Is that too soon? Is that . . ."

Her kókom smiled with her words. "Yes, nósisim, you are even welcome here tomorrow."

Before getting off the phone, Morgan was sure to get directions to her kókom's house, typing them into her phone, and hoping that she would, indeed, get to follow them as early as the next day.

That evening, over supper with Katie and James, Morgan floated the idea of going to see her kókom in Norway House.

"Yes, of course," Katie said. "We can go see your kókom. I think it's important to see her *and* your community."

"How about we let you miss school on Friday next week?"

James said. "That way we can head out early in the morning, get there midafternoon, and we'll have the whole weekend."

Katie already had her phone out. "I just googled it—there's a hotel we can stay at. We wouldn't want to impose on your kókom," she said. "We can spend time with her—hopefully she'll be okay with all of us coming—and tour around the reserve, too. See all the sights."

Morgan looked across the table to see that Eli's expression was disappointed, and his eyes were on his dinner plate.

"It's not, like, a museum exhibit, Katie," she said. "We're not sightseeing, as though it's a vacation or something. It's my home."

Morgan hadn't intended to be snarky. She knew that Katie hadn't meant it that way, and, as usual, she only wanted the best for Morgan. Katie so desperately wanted to do the right thing all the time. Now she was wishing that she'd just let it slide. Being rude wouldn't help convince Katie and James to take them tomorrow, not next week. And it had to be tomorrow. If they waited a week, their relatives in Misewa would be waiting for them . . . Morgan didn't even want to do the Misewa Math. It would be a super long time. Years. She couldn't stand the thought of being away from them for that long. And that was assuming they'd find a portal at all.

Emily's parents had agreed to let *her* go. They were just waiting on a call from Katie and James to work out details and, according to Emily, make sure they were comfortable with the plan.

"It's a good thing I travel for hockey so much," Emily had said. "They're pretty used to me going away with other kids' parents."

"I'm sorry," Morgan said to Katie now. "I really didn't mean to talk to you like that for the billionth time. It's just . . ." She buried her face in her hands. "It's been a really long day."

"No, you're right," Katie said. "I only meant that we can see the places that are important to your family."

"I want to see where I lived." Morgan came up for air. "Where my mom lived. Where my kókom lives." She played with her dinner, using her fork to make shapes out of her mashed potatoes. "It's just that . . ." She started, but then shook her head. "Never mind."

"No," James said, "come on now. It's obviously something. Tell us."

"We'll do whatever we can for you, you know that," Katie said.

Morgan had made a very sloppy, very disfigured mashed potato giant. To her, it looked more like Barney than Mistapew. She smooshed the figure with her fork.

"It's just that, I feel like I need to be there now. I feel, like, drawn there." *Here goes nothing*, Morgan thought. "Can we go this weekend? Emily's parents said that she could go, too. She's already going to sleep over tonight."

"Yes, but Morgan," James said, "Emily sleeping over tonight isn't the same as traveling . . . how far is it?"

"About seven or eight hours," Katie said.

"Traveling seven or eight hours north tomorrow and coming back the next day," James said.

"If you were going to let us miss school on Friday, couldn't we maybe miss school on Monday, instead?" Morgan suggested.

All of this was so awkward for her. She was being whiny now and she hated it. Sure, she cried a lot. She got angry easily. But whiny really wasn't how she saw herself. This was what pulling out all the stops looked like.

"Maybe we should just . . ." Katie whispered to James, who was clearly the holdout.

"I'm on call this weekend," James whispered back. "I kind of think I should be there if we're going to take her."

"I'm sure it won't be the only time we go up north," Katie said.

They were still talking as though Morgan and Eli weren't there. Morgan was listening with great interest and rising optimism. She glanced at Eli and saw that he was, too. He'd looked up from his dinner plate. Things seemed to be leaning in the direction the siblings wanted them to lean. Leaning five hundred miles north towards her home community, to be exact.

"You hate driving," James said.

"I can manage, for something this important," Katie said.

With that, she turned to Morgan, who was sitting so far forward on the edge of her chair that her sweater very nearly had mashed potatoes on it. "Does your . . . kókom . . . know that we might be coming?"

"My kókom said I'm always welcome there because it's my home," Morgan said proudly. "I called her today."

Katie looked at James, who sighed, then nodded at Katie. "How can you argue with that?" he asked.

"That settles it," Katie said. "If we leave early tomorrow morning, we'll get there after lunch and we'll have the rest of the day and all of Sunday. Even the whole morning on Monday!"

"So . . . we can go?" Morgan asked excitedly.

"Yes," Katie said, "we can go."

TWENTY-FIVE

Emily arrived late on Friday evening, after packing, and when she got to the house, she and Morgan talked deep into the night. Soon, after only a few hours of sleep, it was time to get up. They didn't even have breakfast; Katie planned to stop at a drive-through on the way out of the city, and she packed snacks for the rest of the drive. Morgan should have been exhausted, but instead she felt energized. So much lay ahead: answers to questions she'd wondered about for a long time, and another quest, but on earth for once. Where there were no groundlings, there was no endless winter, but maybe there would be bears.

And hopefully bigfoot.

There was nothing special about the first couple of hours on the road. It was a drive through the prairies, after all, which was like being stuck in *Groundhog Day*: the land was relentlessly flat and unremarkable. Small towns came and went like fleeting thoughts, in among farmers' fields that seemed to go on forever. They played I Spy to stave off boredom, they tried to convince Katie to play songs they liked, they played 21 Questions, they played on their phones when they had service and they read when they didn't.

After those first couple of hours, the scenery changed, with lush forests and vast lakes replacing the endless farmland. The leaves in the early autumn looked as though they had been painted with bright oranges and reds and yellows, and the water mirrored the sky. The road was empty, as if the highway had been closed for all but them so they could enjoy the beauty of the north without distraction.

The farther north they got, the more remote it felt, and the more wildlife they saw. A fox trotted alongside the highway, two moose grazed at the tree line, an eagle landed in its nest high at the top of a tree, and a mother bear and her cubs walked into the open, and then back into the safety of the forest when they heard the vehicle approaching. Nothing changed for another few hours, and Morgan didn't want it to—this world was so new to her. Then they came upon a break in their isolation, a First Nations community that Eli had passed through many times but nobody else in the car had heard of.

The highway—which had till now been straight, as though shot from a bow—wound through the community like the river that meandered through the southern woods. There were houses to their left, some spaced apart and some built close together. Many were prefab houses, others were trailers. On the right was first a restaurant and gas station, then a church, a community center, and an Elders' residence attached to a health clinic.

"They've got, like, everything that a town would have," Morgan observed.

"Yeah," Eli said. "Norway House even has a mall."

"What's in the mall?" Emily asked.

"Lots of stuff. There's a post office, a bank, a coffee shop, a gift shop, a grocery store . . ."

"Does the grocery store have everything we have in the city?" Katie asked. "We could pick up some things for supper."

"Sure, if you want to pay more," Eli said. "Lots more."

"Why would it be so much more?" Morgan asked.

"I guess because it costs more to ship things up to remote communities," Eli said. "That's what my grandfather told me. Like, what do you pay for a bag of apples at Safeway, Katie?"

She thought about it for a moment. "I'm not sure. Maybe eight dollars for a bag?"

"So," Eli said, "a bag of apples at the store in Norway House might be twenty dollars or something."

"Twenty dollars!?" Morgan said, appalled. "That's crazy."

"What's crazier is that a bag of chips costs the same as it does in the city. Junk food's always less expensive," Eli said. "That's why my grandfather and I go onto the land to get whatever food we can. It's healthier, and it's cheaper."

They decided they would have dinner at the diner near the hotel in Norway House, and avoid going to the grocery store.

They crossed over a bridge where, below, a wide rushing river fed into an enormous lake called Lake Winnipeg. The highway turned sharply left, then right, and there were fewer houses after each bend, as though the road were shedding the community. Soon, the reserve was behind them, and the forest reintroduced itself.

After a while, short cliff faces and rocky terrain appeared as frequently as trees, an indication that they'd traveled deep into the Boreal Shield, the massive area stretching over two thousand miles across northern Canada, where the boreal forest and the Canadian Shield overlap. Morgan found this land just as pretty as the densely forested areas. On the cliff faces of the little mountains (as she called them), Morgan spotted spray-paint images, kind of like graffiti, just like you'd see on train cars. There were pictures of sacred animals (eagles, turtles, bears, beavers); of people who, she thought, might have been killed on the highway; and initials within hearts, like tattoos. Inuksuit—structures made of stones piled on top of each other—appeared just as frequently, placed on cliff tops or on flat surfaces that jutted out from the cliff faces. Muskwa used to tell Morgan that a legend could change, based on who was telling it and how they interpreted its meaning, but no matter how it was told, the beauty of it remained. Morgan thought the inuksuit were like that; they looked similar, but each held its own unique charm.

The road to Norway House from Winnipeg was in the shape of a candy cane. You drove straight up north, then you turned right to go east, and finally right to go south one last time, at which point you continued for a hundred miles before arriving in the community. After a long trip, Katie, who'd driven every mile happily, albeit with the help of a few coffees, took that last right. Within half an hour they were passing the turnoff to Cross Lake, Eli's home community, and Morgan noticed Eli staring longingly out the window.

She felt awful for a long while after that, because they'd come all this way for her, and there was his home, close but agonizingly far. Katie glanced back at Eli when she saw the sign for Cross Lake, and she looked troubled, too.

"I'm sorry, Eli," she said. "If I could take you there, I would, but it's just not allowed right now."

"Yeah," Eli said, despondently. "I know."

Eli looked out the rear window, at the turnoff to his community, long after they'd passed it by.

Long after it had disappeared in the distance.

Eventually, they came to the ferry crossing that would take them across the Nelson River. From there, Norway House was only twenty minutes away. The ferry was on the other side of the river at the moment, and they had to wait. Emily and Katie chatted together in the front seat as they watched the water. Emily was getting along well with Morgan's foster mother; Morgan suspected Emily got along well with most people. She thought about how Arik and Emily couldn't stop talking together on their walk through the northern woods.

Morgan glanced over at Eli, who was sitting beside her in the backseat. He had been slumped over, head buried in his hoodie, ever since they'd passed Cross Lake. Katie's words echoed in Morgan's mind: *It's just not allowed right now.*

"Why can Katie get my mother's phone number, but we can't visit your reserve?" Morgan asked Eli softly, as Katie and Emily continued to chat in the front seat. "Why'd they take you away?"

It was a hard question. Morgan knew that. She had never asked him why he'd been apprehended by the foster care system before, but Eli knew what had happened to Morgan, and this seemed the right time to find out. She wasn't sure if he would even answer her. Maybe it was being so close to his community, so close to the memories, or maybe it was because they'd grown close to each other. Whatever the reason, Eli surprised her and said, "It's kind of simple. I mean, what happened. The reason why they took me, I guess that's not as simple."

"I don't think it's that simple for me, either," Morgan said, at once encouraging him and trying to comfort him.

"The RCMP pulled my dad over because they said he had expired plates," Eli said. "My dad got upset because they made him get out of the car, made him put his hands on the hood, stuff like that. He was like, 'You guys need to stop harassing me.' I guess it wasn't the first time they'd pulled him over. I was in the backseat, watching everything. My mom got out to try and calm everybody down, but the next thing I knew, one of the RCMP guys was tackling my dad, and he wasn't even doing anything. They arrested both my parents."

Eli hid his face, rubbed his cheeks with his hoodie, then came out of hiding. He hadn't quite succeeded in wiping the tears away.

"The next day, some people took me away from my grand-father's place." He shrugged. "That was that."

It seemed as though Eli, staring blankly at Morgan, was *there* now, not looking at his sister but watching his parents get arrested. Katie and Emily stopped talking. Their attention was on Eli. The ferry had almost arrived.

"I'm sorry, Eli," Morgan said. "I'm so sorry. I didn't know."

"If I could take you home, I would," Katie said. "Your parents didn't deserve . . . you didn't deserve . . ."

Vehicles were driving on to the ferry now. A car behind them honked, but Katie wouldn't drive up just yet. She turned in her seat to look right at Eli, and she shook her head. It was the first time Morgan had seen her look angry.

"If I could take you home, I would," she repeated. And then she drove forward, and they were on the ferry.

Halfway across, probably desperate to leave the memory behind, Eli poked Morgan on the arm, and pointed up the river.

"It's that way," he whispered. "Where they saw Mistapew."

Morgan looked where Eli was pointing, following the river as it rushed towards Cross Lake, splitting to wind around small islands then coming back together as though not wanting to be torn apart. The trees that lined the shore were thick, and so close together you couldn't see deep into the forest. Not from where they were. She wondered if, somewhere in there—somewhere hidden so well that it had remained a secret, that its very existence had been passed off as a hoax—there really was a bigfoot.

They were about to find out.

TWENTY-SIX

They arrived in Norway House just before 3:00 p.m. The reserve was pretty much what Morgan had expected, based on Eli's description of First Nations communities. They drove past houses built in little clusters off the road, as though mindful not to disturb the densely forested area. Generations of relatives typically lived in these groupings—grandparents in one, parents and their children in another, aunties and uncles and cousins in another. And the center of the community looked like any other town they'd driven through in rural Manitoba. There was a baseball diamond, a multiplex movie theater, a modern-looking school, the mall, a gas station, and then the hotel they'd be staying in.

Morgan's kókom's house was at the end of a short field, and it backed onto the woods. There were no addresses, so the directions she'd given Morgan weren't much more specific than that. They had to follow the main street to the right, where they'd pass the old cemetery, and then after a few more houses they'd find the field. After stopping on the shoulder of the road, they could walk across the grass to get to her place. She didn't have a driveway.

"There are already too many roads to too many places these days," she'd said.

The plan was to stop by first thing Sunday morning for breakfast—her kókom had promised to prepare a feast for them—but, to make sure they knew where they were going, the group decided to drive past the bungalow now.

The directions made perfect sense. They kept to the right, passed an oval field where children were playing soccer, a women's shelter, a daycare, and then, finally, the old cemetery. The cemetery was sadly unkempt, as though it were too hard to visit the dead. The grass was long and grew over the headstones. A number of graves had white crosses that looked weathered and unmarked. Others were just mounds protruding from the earth. On the opposite side of the old cemetery was a shimmering lake that was impossibly beautiful. Morgan decided that each glitter of light was a soul dancing.

And then at last they saw the field that Morgan's kókom had mentioned. It was relatively small, about half the size of a football field, and across it, nestled against the tree line, was a burgundy bungalow. Facing them, on the east side of the house, there was nothing more than a window. Of course, Morgan had never been to Norway House before, and so certainly had never seen the house before, but it looked familiar to her straight away. She could feel the grass, cool beneath her feet, the long blades brushing against her shins. She could feel the breeze. She could feel her hand against the thin wall of the prefab dwelling. She could see inside the window, in her mind's eye. There was a rocking chair. A side table. A lamp. And a woman, rocking her baby. She didn't take her eyes off it until they'd passed by, following the main street back around the other way, towards the hotel.

"I think that was it, wasn't it?" Katie asked. "That little burgundy house."

"It was," Morgan said. "That was the place."

It was almost 4:00 p.m. when they finished checking into the hotel, a two-story building with no more than twenty rooms. Morgan guessed the community didn't always get a lot of visitors. When they were given keys for their rooms, actual keys, she noticed that there were a number of them still hanging from little hooks on the wall, waiting to be claimed. Katie had reserved three rooms, because they were relatively inexpensive. Katie got one room, Morgan and Emily shared another, and Eli was in his own. "It's because I'm way more mature," he teased Morgan. Katie gave them an hour to get settled, and at 5:00 p.m. they met in the lobby to go for supper.

They all ordered hamburgers and french fries that came with sides of coleslaw that nobody touched.

"Has anybody ever eaten a side of coleslaw at a restaurant?" Morgan asked, before digging into the large and greasy burger.

It was a good counterbalance to the healthy snacks Katie

had packed for the drive, which consisted of nuts, apples, oranges, crackers and hummus, and bottled smoothies. Aside from Morgan's question—to which Emily replied, "I'm sure it's happened, but I've never seen it"—dinner was quiet and efficient. Ordering, waiting for the food, and eating it took less than an hour, and by 6:00 p.m. they were walking across the parking lot back towards the hotel.

"Do you guys want to see more of the community tonight?" Katie asked.

She didn't sound overly excited at the prospect of exploring the reserve. And who could blame her, since she'd spent most of the day driving? Of course, the kids had never planned on any sort of tour. At least not tonight. So Katie's lack of energy suited them fine. They had other, more important plans. It was November, so by then it was already beginning to get dark. Before night fell, they wanted to head towards the trapline.

"Honestly, I'm pretty wiped out," Morgan said. "And I'm already nervous about tomorrow. I think I just want to read or something."

"She brought about five fantasy books, in case anybody was wondering," Eli said.

"You don't say," Emily teased. Morgan, when she wasn't in school, or on an adventure in a different reality, almost always had a fantasy book in her hand.

"I've been here lots of times," Eli said. "I'm probably just going to draw."

"Dude," Emily said to Eli, "we could be in the most exotic place in the world and you'd have your head in that drawing pad."

"To draw the most exotic place in the world so that I don't forget what it looks like."

"Isn't that what Instagram is for?"

"I don't need likes," Eli said. "And to me, a drawing means more than a photograph."

They went back to their rooms, after making a plan with Katie to be up early the next morning. Morgan had expected her to make them swear to stay in their rooms and not get up to any mischief, but Katie must have been too tired to even think about it, so at least Morgan wouldn't have to break a promise.

They'd all stuffed warmer clothing into their backpacks in preparation for the journey into the bush. They'd also brought, collectively, a flashlight, some snacks, matches to start a fire, and a beach tent, which was the only tent Emily could fit into her backpack. If they had to sleep in the bush that night for whatever reason, it would be in a tent smaller than the sweat lodge they'd built in the northern woods.

"I guess we'll all be cuddling," Emily had joked.

The girls left their hotel room, snuck past Katie's room without incident, and met Eli outside in the parking lot. It was time for another adventure.

TWENTY-SEVEN

"So, what now?" Morgan asked.

She'd come up with the general plan. They would go to where the bigfoot had been spotted, find the portal it used to travel from one reality to another, and get back to Askí. It was a good plan, but admittedly light on details. First and foremost, Morgan asked, how were they going to get to the trapline? Walk? They were loitering outside the hotel now, but they couldn't stay there for long. What if Katie decided to go for a walk?

"Follow me," Eli said, and he took off running towards the main street they'd traveled on earlier.

The trio ran up the street, towards the part of the community where the houses were built shoulder to shoulder. When they came to the spot where Morgan's kókom had instructed them to go to the right, Eli kept going straight for awhile, then he veered off to the left and headed towards the water. Eli stopped by the lake, where boats were lined up along the shore.

Nobody was around but them.

"I couldn't help but notice," Morgan said, "that we kind of went the wrong way." She pointed north. "Isn't the trapline that way?"

"You asked how we're going to get to the trapline." Eli pointed at the boats. "That's how."

"You want to steal a boat?" Emily asked.

"Did we bring one?" Eli asked. "I didn't notice."

"Look who grew an attitude!" Emily said.

"Brother," Morgan said, "it's my first time visiting my home community, and you want us to take something that isn't ours?"

"People borrow each other's boats all the time on my reserve," Eli said.

"Yeah, but they probably let the other person know," Morgan said.

"There has to be another way," Emily said. "If we get caught we'll be in so much trouble. Not to mention that my parents would literally kill me. Like, my hockey season would be over."

"There isn't another way," Eli said. "We can't drive there, we can't swim there, we can't walk there. We have to borrow a boat. *Borrow*. Nobody's going out at this time of night. Nobody'll even know a boat is gone."

"I'd honestly rather take Katie's car and hope she doesn't catch us," Morgan said. "One of the only nice things a foster parent did for me at one home was take me driving on a gravel road. I could totally—"

"Katie has the keys in her room," Emily said. "How would we get them?"

"Right." Morgan slapped herself on her forehead. "Duh." Morgan started to think of a new plan. A car key heist. They'd have to distract Katie, sneak into her room, take her keys, and drive down the highway to a place where they could get out and hike through the woods to the trapline.

"The road's too far from the trapline anyway," Eli said, as though reading Morgan's mind. "We'd never make it in time and get back to the community for breakfast tomorrow."

"Darn it!" Morgan kicked a large stone and watched it skip along the ground, then land in the water. It was the only way she could display her frustration short of tearing her hair out. "So that's it. We take a boat or we don't have a chance of getting back to Askí. Good to know."

"Look," Emily said, "I guess . . ." She sighed deeply. Morgan thought she was probably imagining her hockey season vanishing. "I'll go. If you really need to do this, let's do this."

"But your parents," Morgan said.

"They won't *literally* kill me, you know," Emily joked. "Just figuratively. And I know how much this place means to you, Morg. If there's a chance we can get back there, and you want to take that chance, I'll take that chance, too."

"Really?" Morgan said.

"Yeah," Emily said. "You'd do the same for me."

Emily was right. Morgan would do the same for her. But she didn't have as much to lose as Emily did. What could Katie and James do—take away her books? How did she ever deserve Emily? She gave her the biggest hug she'd ever given her.

"Thank you," Morgan said.

Emily patted her on the back after a few seconds and gently pushed her off. "As much as I love hugging you, and as much as I meant everything I just said, if I could avoid getting caught that would be awesome. So, we should go."

"Yep," Morgan said. Then she turned towards Eli. "Okay, I guess we're *borrowing* a boat."

Eli started to check the vessels for one that had an outboard motor that you pulled to start—no key required. "It's not like this is the first time we've taken a boat anyway," he said.

While Morgan watched Eli go from boat to boat under the darkening sky, she remembered their first visit to the North Country. There, they'd come up with an elaborate plan, far more detailed than this one, to steal Mason's canoe. The good thing about taking *this* boat was that there wouldn't be anybody firing arrows at them during their getaway.

Once Eli found a suitable boat, he and Morgan climbed in. Eli started the motor. Emily pushed the boat into the lake, jumped in to join the other two, and they were on their way.

On the water, it was easy to forget the urgency of their mission. Bobbing up and down on the waves, surrounded by trees, had a calming effect. It helped that Eli was allowing the current to move them at first, not wanting to rev the engine and alert community members that there was a boat in the water. But even when they were clear of Norway House and Eli felt comfortable going fast, Morgan still felt calm. She was enjoying the soothing effect of the wind rushing against her face.

It wasn't long before they passed the ferry crossing. At that point, Eli really picked up speed, and it felt as though the boat was gliding over the river's surface. Morgan was impressed by how skillfully Eli handled the boat in the dark, how fluidly he steered it down particular routes when the river branched off in different directions, how he knew exactly where he needed to go to avoid large rocks underneath the surface that might damage the hull. They'd come upon an island that rose high above the water, with cliff faces like the ones they'd seen from the highway, and Eli coaxed the boat smoothly around it. They found themselves headed towards what looked like open water, at least half a mile wide, and Eli just wove to the right and left, avoiding unseen impediments that might have cut their journey short. He had traveled the same route countless times, and he knew exactly how to get them to the trapline safely. It made Morgan happy to know that he hadn't forgotten. And when she looked away from the swift water and the dense forest at the shoreline, she saw, in the moonlight, contentment on his face, too.

And so, when the river opened up into a small lake and Eli cut the engine to allow the boat to drift ashore near a clearing, Morgan decided that, whether or not they found a portal, it would be okay. Eli looked as assured and strong as he did on Askí, and Morgan felt a familiar pull herself. It reminded her of the feeling she had when stepping through the portal in the Great Tree, what felt like a lifetime ago.

The aluminum hull scraped against the round white rocks on the shore. Emily jumped out first with the rope, and when Eli and Morgan had pulled the boat up onto the shore she tied it to a tree to secure it. Then, Morgan and Emily followed Eli up an incline towards a clearing surrounded by forest: the trapline.

In the middle of the clearing was a firepit dug into the earth and encircled by rocks, and those rocks were further encircled by four thick logs. Off to the side, near the tree line, was a pile of chopped wood covered by a tarp to keep it dry. As soon as they came to the firepit, Eli went off to gather smaller branches to start a fire. Emily and Morgan, meanwhile, sat together on a log and watched Eli work, with little else they could do at the moment. Morgan would have offered to help build the fire, but that had been Eli's job on Askí, and he looked pleased to be doing the task now.

"You know," Eli said, approaching the firepit with an armful of dry branches cradled in his arms, "usually the women did most of the work around the camp, on the trapline. I mean, traditionally. The men would be off checking snares, resetting them, that kind of stuff."

"Look at us, breaking gender norms to pieces!" Emily chuckled.

"Yeah, you just keep it up, Eli, we're good," Morgan said.

"It's about time women got to watch a man work," Emily said.

"True." Morgan laughed, but she added, "Working the trapline is pretty hard, though, to be honest. I've done it, with Ochek and Arik."

"Then you've earned a break, wouldn't you say?"

"I guess I have, Houldsy."

The plan was to build a fire for warmth, but also as a beacon, so when they hiked into the bush it would be easy to navigate their way back. Eli thought he'd be able to find his way around in the dark, but better safe than sorry. And before heading out into the bush, they'd have a quick snack, building up energy for what could prove to be a difficult trek around the area, searching for a portal. Nobody had any idea how long the search might take, or even what a portal might look like. Were they always trees? Because if that was the case, the portal could be in any one of a thousand on the trapline. How were they to find one specific tree? Did they look for the biggest, tallest tree? A Great Tree, here on earth? Or, if the portal was something else, what would it be? A cliff face behind one of the many waterfalls Eli had spoken about? He had said once that little people lived in caves behind waterfalls. Was there magic there?

The more she tossed these questions around in her mind, the more unlikely it seemed to Morgan that this expedition would bring them to Askí. It seemed more likely that this place, this trapline, would have to be their new Misewa, even without their animal-being family.

Eli was stuffing twigs and birch bark into the neat stack of wood he'd constructed in the firepit. He was about to light the kindling when he stopped suddenly and froze.

"Did you hear that?" he whispered.

"Hear what?" Emily asked.

"I honestly don't hear anything," Morgan said.

"Listen," he said.

Eli hadn't snuffed the match. The flame was flickering in a slight breeze, and burning closer and closer to his thumb and index finger. He didn't notice, but Morgan did, and she blew it out. The little light the match had offered was gone. Out there on the land, there was only the soft white light of the stars and moon.

Eli took out the flashlight and shone it into the bush. Morgan was starting to freak out. So was Emily. They grabbed each other's hands.

"There aren't, like, groundlings on earth, right?" Morgan asked. "That's just a northern woods kind of thing."

"It's not groundlings," Eli said. "The way you described them? There's nothing like that out here. I've been on the trapline enough times to know that."

"Is it . . . bigfoot? He's sneaky, isn't he?" Emily asked.

There was a rustling in the bush to their left, and Eli pointed the flashlight there. They saw movement. They heard a low growl. Morgan tried to remember if she'd ever heard Mistapew growl. The giant had for sure roared. If he'd roared, then he could definitely growl. But Eli didn't run. He stood up and took a few steps towards where the bush was shaking. There was another growl, then Eli whistled and dropped to his knees. Something barked, then burst into the clearing, racing towards Eli. He dropped the flashlight. When he did, the light hit the animal, revealing copper fur.

"Eli, run!" Emily said, getting ready to leap towards Eli to protect him.

But Morgan, who was still holding Emily's hand, pulled her back.

"No," she said, "don't."

The animal jumped at Eli and tackled him to the ground. They started to roll around on the grass. The dog was barking like crazy.

Eli was laughing, and saying, over and over, "Good boy! Good boy!"

"I'm so confused," Emily said.

"That's Eli's dog." Morgan watched the two friends wrestle each other all over the clearing. She remembered Eli telling her about his dog, who lived on the trapline. "That's Red."

TWENTY-EIGHT

From that time on, Red, a big copper-haired, curly tailed mutt, would not leave Eli's side, and Eli, boyish and overjoyed, would not leave Red's. He finished making the fire, lighting the birch bark with a second match, and they sat on the logs eating the snacks they'd brought. Eli gave half of his food to Red, who greedily devoured the treat.

"What does he eat when he's out here?" Emily asked.

"Whatever he catches," Eli said, "just like everybody else who lives on the trapline. I don't think he's hungry too often, though." He patted the dog on the head. "You're a good hunter, aren't you, boy?"

Red wagged his tail furiously, which earned him a bit of Morgan's snack. She tossed it to him and he caught it in midair. Not only was he a good hunter, but he could do tricks! Morgan could see instantly why Eli had missed the dog so much. It wasn't just that he was able to sustain himself on the land or catch food in the air; Morgan saw that he was good-natured. He looked like he was always smiling, and not just with his mouth, but with his eyes. *How much Arik would love him, too!* Morgan thought. If an atim had not been in Misewa for years, Red would be the perfect one to bring to the village.

First, of course, they needed to get there.

Morgan checked the time on her phone and saw that it was getting late. They could only look for the portal for so long, and if they found it, they wouldn't have much time to spend in Askí; they'd have to be back in Norway House before 6:00 a.m. Morgan had no idea when Katie might get up and check on them—maybe she'd even check on them in the night—and she had no idea when the boat owner might notice their property was gone.

"We'd better start looking," Morgan said, getting to her feet.

The others stood up with her.

"You're probably right," Eli said.

Emily scanned the forest all around the clearing. It was relatively small—only big enough for a couple of tents—but the woods were massive, and held endless possibilities.

"Where do we even start?" she asked, sounding overwhelmed. "I think we may have underestimated how big the search area is."

"Not necessarily," Eli said. "When people used to live on traplines—when we *still* go out on the land—there are patterns. We stay in certain places. Animals have patterns, just like people. They move, but not everywhere, just to particular areas. This bigfoot must have a pattern."

"So, what particular areas would it be in?" Emily asked.

"Where was it in that video?" Morgan asked.

"Right here," Eli said. He pointed out over the water. "They were fishing right there, and that's where they filmed it from. It walked right across this clearing."

"So, like, if this is where they filmed it, this is where we look," Morgan said. "It's all we have time for."

"Okay, but this place is pretty huge itself," Emily said. "Not to be negative."

"It walked . . ." Morgan tried to remember the video as best she could. "It walked across this way, then it went into the bush around there, I think." She motioned to the bush, then asked Eli, "What's back there? Anything? Or is it all just . . . more trees?"

"No, not *just,*" Eli said. "About half a mile in that direction there's a big lake. I used to walk around it, swim in it . . . maybe . . ."

"It's something to go on," Emily said.

"Other than checking every single tree that's wide enough for a giant to fit through," Morgan said, and then she added, "Come to think of it, though, that actually might not be all that many trees!"

Eli crouched beside Red and stroked his back. "What do you think, boy? Should we try it?"

Red barked one single time, then Morgan and Emily watched as Eli, as though jolted into movement, walked to the edge of the forest and stood there, peering through the trees and bush. He stayed there until the girls decided to join him. Morgan wondered if he'd seen something, if maybe the bigfoot had walked by.

"Eli," she whispered, "what're you doing?"

"I felt . . ."

Eli held his hand out in a particular direction, fingers spread apart.

"You felt what?" Emily asked.

"That if the bigfoot is here, he's somewhere near the water," Eli said, trance-like. "But I felt something else, too. Something . . . elusive."

"Okay, Obi-Wan in *The Phantom Menace*." Morgan chortled. "At least quote a good Star Wars movie. And when did you see that movie, anyway?"

"I wasn't quoting a movie." Eli locked eyes with Morgan, and he was deadly serious. "The portal's there. I can feel it."

"You can . . . feel it," Morgan repeated.

"I can feel it, and I know where it is," Eli said. "Let's go."

Without hesitating a moment longer, Eli walked into the forest with Red. Morgan and Emily exchanged a look, shrugged at the same time, then followed him.

Eli trekked through the bush with purpose, and it reminded Morgan of Mihko or Ochek. It reminded her, as well, of how hard it had always been for her to keep up with those two. And Emily was having a tougher time than Morgan. Morgan guessed that even though Emily was in better shape, Morgan had done way more walking through the bush. That's why her moccasins were worn out. She liked that she had to make sure not to get too far ahead of Emily—but she had to try to keep Eli in sight, too. It was a good thing they'd found Red, who was so excited to be hiking with Eli that he was barking all the time. When they got too far in front, Morgan and Emily just followed the sound of Red.

If Morgan hadn't known any better, she would have thought they were walking through the southern woods on Askí. The trees towered high above, sturdy, vibrant, and full. The sky was clear; the stars were bright and millions strong. The air was fresh and crisp, as refreshing as the stream they'd found by Mistapew's cave. Morgan was sure that if she listened hard enough, she would be able to hear the heartbeat of mother earth. When she was in the North Country, she used to think that there was no place like it on earth. The sky never so clear. The waters never so quick and cool. The land never so alive.

Turned out, she was wrong.

Morgan, then Emily, caught up to Eli, who'd stopped at the lake he'd described earlier. It was more like a large pond, in the shape of a kidney, protected by the forest. The water mirrored the night sky so perfectly that if you were to jump into it, you might think for a moment that you'd fallen to the stars. That is, until Red leapt into it and paddled around. The kids laughed watching the dog, until he came ashore and shook himself dry. Then they got back to the matter at hand.

"You know where you're going," Morgan said. "So, where to now?"

Eli held out his hand again, then began walking east, around the water. Morgan and Emily followed him. About halfway around, he stopped at a beaten-down path that led deeper into the woods.

"In here," he said.

They followed the path for several minutes, and it was as though they were being tested. The trail wasn't easy. It led them up steep inclines where they had to use exposed roots to pull themselves up. It took them down embankments where they were forced to inch their way down so as not to fall and roll all the way to the bottom. It brought them through thick underbrush and over felled trees, and the journey felt as though it took hours, but when Morgan checked her phone it had been less than twenty minutes. Twenty minutes until they came upon a clearing no bigger than her bedroom, and in the middle of it, a boulder almost as tall as her.

Morgan thought at first that it was just the darkness that made it look black, but when Eli shone his flashlight on it, it remained as black as obsidian. Eli led them around the boulder, illuminating it for all of them. Half of the boulder was rough, full of shallow fissures, slight ridges, and other imperfections. But the other half was smooth and flat like a wall, and on the ground at this side of the boulder was a pile of pointed white rocks.

Eli put his hand against the boulder and closed his eyes. "This is the portal," he said.

Emily approached the flat side of the boulder and knocked on it. "This is the portal? For real?" She knocked on it a second time, and then, as though she were in a hockey game, checked it with her shoulder. Morgan wondered if she expected to fall through it into another reality or something.

"I don't think it works that way," Morgan said, and she couldn't hold in a chuckle.

Emily rubbed her shoulder, grimacing. "So how does it work?"

"Probably how the other one worked." Eli crouched down and picked up one of the white rocks. He ran it along the flat black surface and it left a clear white stroke behind. "I bet the bigfoot draws pictures with these rocks, and we'll have to do the same."

"So what do you draw? The Barren Grounds?" Emily asked.

"No," Eli said. "I don't think so. That's not what I see, anyway."

Morgan's heart sank. Did that mean they couldn't go back to Aski? Did the portal open to a different reality altogether? Or, allowing herself to feel hopeful, did the portal open to Aski, but to another part of that world? But then, where? How big was Aski, anyway? As big as earth? What if they ended up so far away that they had to walk . . . well, there was no way they could walk all the way around the world. She was pretty sure there were no cars or airplanes on Aski. How would they get to Misewa? They couldn't. They'd have to come back and try to find another portal somewhere else. Or maybe it really would open into the North Country? Anywhere in the North Country would be walking distance to the village.

"What do you see?" Morgan asked Eli.

"Life everywhere," Eli said. "Animals, birds, fish jumping out of the river."

So, there's a river, Morgan thought. So far, it was the only mildly specific thing, and even then, it wasn't really specific.

Eli went on. "There's a forest, but it's not the southern or northern woods. I don't recognize it. There are thin trees, and they're tall. Redwoods, I think. And sequoias.

Lots of them. I feel so small around them. It's like the forest is for giants. The brush is so thick and green."

Eli started to draw, and the picture he was creating looked exactly like what he had recited to the girls. There were impossibly tall trees, and bush and underbrush so thick Morgan wondered how they'd walk through it. There was no path. But that was okay, they could forge one. Was this forest, the one Eli was illustrating, even in Askí? She asked him that, because she'd never seen anything like it.

"I don't know," Eli said. "I think so. I feel like it is."

"You're feeling a lot of things," Emily pointed out. She turned to Morgan. "Was he always like this? Like, could he see worlds, and could he just . . . you know . . . *feel* portals? Because you know how people sometimes have those rods and they swing them around and it leads them to water? Eli just did the same thing, only without a rod, and instead of water he went right to this big boulder."

"He could see things," Morgan said. "That's how we went to Askí the first time. He just drew the Barren Grounds, and Ochek. But he couldn't find portals. Maybe . . ." She thought of how Eli's soul had been stuck in the rock. The Stone Child. She thought of how Kihiw had been stuck in the Great Tree, and how Eli knew it. She thought of how Mistapew placed souls into trees and stones. Had being trapped in the moon stone by Mistapew opened an ability to find portals? To find souls? "Maybe being stuck in that rock changed him."

"It wouldn't be the weirdest thing that's happened to us recently," Emily said. "He did find the portal. If it were science class, I'd say the hypothesis has been proven."

"There's no evidence to prove otherwise, that's for sure," Morgan said.

She wasn't sure whether Eli had heard their conversation. He was drawing as though possessed, and the picture was coming together quickly and clearly. Morgan and Emily quieted down and let him work. It was entrancing, watching Eli's hands move so quickly but still so precisely. Finishing a tree here, filling in some brush there. Even Red had stopped barking, as though he could appreciate his master's artistry. Then, finally, Eli made one last stroke, and dropped the white stone to the ground.

As soon as that stroke had been made, Eli's drawing began to cave in towards the middle of the flat surface, where a vortex formed. Red's ears flattened and he ran behind Eli, cowering there, his tail tucked between his legs. Eli crouched down and began to pet him, trying to settle him down. As more of the drawing spilled into the swirling hole, it grew until it took up the entire surface of the boulder. Large enough for the kids to walk through. And large enough to see through it, where everything Eli had drawn was alive. The forest with its thin, tall trees waited for them in the middle of the day. Warm air rushed through the portal, inviting them forward. Eli stood and walked right up to it.

"Come on, boy," he said to his dog, motioning for him to follow by patting his thigh, "it's okay."

Red army-crawled to Eli, until he was by Eli's side. Once there, and feeling safe, he straightened up. Eli rewarded him with a pat on the head, and then boy and dog were the first to go through the opening, taking a few cautious steps before running into the forest, Red barking happily while darting this way and that, inspecting the new land.

Morgan and Emily followed close behind, and once they were all the way through, the portal snapped closed and became a boulder, almost a mirror image of the one they'd found on the trapline. There were even drawing supplies on the ground, but not pointed white stones. Instead, on this side there was a large clay pot filled with ocher. The handle of a brush protruded from the pot.

Red continued his inspection, sniffing every inch of ground, and marking his territory against a couple of trees.

"Guys," Morgan said, "where are we?"

"I don't know," Eli said.

"Me either," Emily said. "Other than in a forest."

Morgan put her arm around Emily. "You know what I like about you?"

"Is it my wit and charm?" Emily asked.

"Your powers of observation," Morgan said.

"Shut up." Emily nudged Morgan's hip with her elbow.

"You guys are cute," Eli said.

"You can shut up, too, bro," Morgan said, reaching over and ruffling Eli's hair.

In the silence that followed, the sounds of nature became louder. Birds flapping their wings sounded like thunder. Wind through leaves sounded like rapturous applause. Deer sprinting gracefully through the forest sounded like a rapidly beating heart. And swift water sounded like blood through the veins of mother earth. They followed the sound of the water, and peered through the trees to find a river no more than fifty yards away.

"The water might tell us where we are," Morgan said, "or at least bring us to where we want to go."

"How so?" Emily asked.

"She's right," Eli said. "There's only one river in the North Country. If we follow it . . ."

"We'll find our way home!" Morgan said, and then she took off towards the river.

She expertly dodged trees, jumped over brush, side-stepped large roots, navigated the natural undulations of the forest floor. She knew Eli and Emily were behind her. She heard their footsteps at her heels. She heard Red barking. She ran harder and faster, and the water began to roar in its closeness.

When she came to the shoreline, Eli and Emily stopped on either side of her. Morgan looked far to the east, then to the west. There it was! In the distance, miles away, she saw the shore on either side of the river rise up to form a canyon—the canyon that ran through the southern woods! She followed the current of the river, as though her eyes were carried along by it, all the way back to where they were. Her eyes stopped when they fell upon a skeleton, its bones whiter than a cloud in a blue sky. Morgan knew that was odd imagery, but she thought of a blue sky because the skeleton had ragged blue cloth covering it.

Then it hit her.

"Oh my god, that's Mason," Morgan said, pointing at the skeleton. "Look at the clothes."

"Mason?" Emily said. "That's what Mahihkan told us, right? He washed up down the river?"

"How far down the river?" Eli asked. "What does that mean?"

Morgan turned around full circle, taking in every detail of the river that rushed past them, the forest they were surrounded by, the remains of the man who'd caused so much trauma in the North Country. She knew exactly where they were.

"It means," she said, "welcome to World's End."

TWENTY-NINE

They gathered by the river, around Mason's skeletal remains. Despite what he'd done, Morgan felt bad for him, and by the looks of Emily and Eli, they did, too. She didn't think anybody deserved to die that way. Greed had consumed him, and greed had brought him to where he was now, washed up on the shore, left there for years after animals and birds had picked him clean.

"What do we do with him?" Emily asked.

"We can't just leave him," Morgan said.

"Morgan's right," Eli said. "Let's bury him."

For the next while, the three kids, and Red, worked to dig a large hole on the shoreline, where the ground was soft. They had no tools, so they had to dig with their hands. Red probably got more done than the three of them combined; he was a very efficient digger. It wasn't a strenuous job but it was tedious, and by the time the hole was deep enough, all their hands were black with mud. They placed Mason's bones in the grave, filled in the hole, then washed their hands in the river. All cleaned up, they gathered again at Mason's final resting place.

"Should somebody say something?" Morgan asked.

"I didn't really know the guy, so I feel unqualified," Emily said. "I mean, is there anything nice to say about him? He's probably responsible for a lot of deaths, right?"

Neither Morgan nor Eli argued with that. Emily was right. Many had died because of the White Time, and that endless season of cold had been caused by Mason. Morgan felt bad for him, but not necessarily sad, and certainly not guilty. After all, moments before he'd plummeted to his death, he'd been aiming an arrow at her. And so it was Eli, in the end, who knelt and laid tobacco on the burial place.

"My grandfather used to tell me something, when we were out on the land together," Eli said. "He wanted me to learn the way of the Cree people, our values, our ways of living. He wanted me to feel pride in who I am. But he also wanted to prepare me, I think. He said once, 'I always worry about the world you're growing up in, nósisim. About what people might do or say to you, because it's a hard world to be Indian in.' He was an old-time Cree, so he still used that word. Anyway, he said, 'But you have to understand that, in the end, everybody is human first. If you make a mistake, you're not making a mistake because you're white or because you're Cree. You're making a mistake because you're a human being. Humans make mistakes.'" Eli stood. "Mason made a mistake, and he was human. We can't change any of that, but I hope he finds peace."

"Everybody makes mistakes," Emily said, then tossed some extra dirt onto the grave.

Morgan did the same, and they all stood there for a few minutes, staring at the rectangular plot they'd made. Eli's words were echoing in Morgan's mind as she stared down at the grave: *I hope he finds peace.* The more she stared at the grave, and the more those words repeated in her mind, the more she began to picture another grave. Her mother's grave. She began to change the "he" in what Eli had said to "she." *I hope she finds peace.* She hoped that her mother found peace before she died. But how could she have?

"She died of loneliness," her kókom had told her.

There was no peace in loneliness. Her mother had dreamed of being with her again, but that had never happened. There was no calm in that sort of quiet. Morgan knelt down, picked up some dirt, and spread it over the ground again.

I hope she finds peace.

Morgan stood up suddenly.

What if I could help her find peace? What if I could find my own?

"What is it?" Emily said, looking at Morgan.

Eli was looking at her, too.

Morgan wasn't looking at either of them. She was staring into World's End, in the direction of the portal. She was thinking about Ochek. She was thinking about *young* Ochek. She was bursting with hope. Her heart was pounding. *Thump. Thump. Thump. Thump. Thump. Thump. Thump.* She put her hand on her chest and felt her heart through her sweater, beating like a drum.

"Do you remember what Arik said?" Morgan asked. "About portals?" She didn't wait for an answer. "They're tied to a certain place. Like, the Great Tree was tied to our attic for some crazy reason. If we'd ever tried to go somewhere else on Askí it wouldn't have worked. But . . ." Morgan started to pace back and forth, her footsteps in sync with her hard, fast heartbeat. "But the portals aren't tied to a certain *time*. That's why we were able to go back and see Ochek when he was a kid."

"That strangely all makes sense to me," Emily said.

"Me too," Eli said. "But what're you saying? You want to use this portal to see Ochek again?"

"No," Morgan said. "I want to use this portal to go back in time . . . on earth."

"Why?"

"This portal is tied to the land between Norway House and Cross Lake," she explained. "My mother lived in Norway House." She stopped pacing. The wind rustling the leaves sounded like rain. The ground underneath her feet, the dirt she could feel through the hole in her moccasin, felt cool and firm. The river was swift and wide, bringing life to the North Country. The air was clean and brisk. She took a deep breath in, then out. "I could give her peace."

By Eli's eyes, Morgan knew that he understood. Still, there were logistics that weren't clear.

"I'll do anything to help you see your mom," Eli said, "but the portal won't open to her house. It'll open to the land. It'll open right where we entered it. Your mom's not going to be there. Why would she be there?"

"I don't know," Morgan said. "I just . . . know. Like, Ochek was there the first time because we told him to be there, but why was young Ochek there? Do you remember what he said? He felt like going for a walk around the northern woods and then sitting by the Great Tree. Who would ever do that?"

"I wouldn't go back around those woods, that's for sure," Emily said.

"What are you saying?" Eli asked.

"Something about these portals, these drawings," Morgan mused. "You knew to draw the Barren Grounds, even though you'd never seen them before. You felt a pull to do it. I felt that same pull when I stepped onto the ground here on Askí. What if . . . what if people, animal beings, feel that same pull to be around where you draw them?"

"She might be around the portal?" Eli said.

"Maybe," Morgan said. "It's worth a try, isn't it?"

Minutes later, they were in front of the boulder and its flat, smooth black surface. An empty canvas. Eli had never painted much with ocher, just a few times in Misewa, but he was confident that he could draw well enough with it to open a portal back to earth. In fact, he thought the brush would allow him to draw rather pretty leaves. When he made this comment, Morgan, who was anxious to find out if the plan to see her mother would work, remarked, "This isn't a drawing contest, Eli. You don't have to be Bob Ross, just paint the damn forest."

"Holy," Eli said, picking up the brush.

"Sorry," Morgan said. "I'm just nervous. It worked to see Ochek, but who says it's going to work to see my mother?"

"There's only one way to find out," Eli said and, with Morgan watching and holding Emily's hand for moral support, he began to paint.

He did paint beautifully. The scene, little by little, came together on the boulder. It looked just like the area they'd left to come to World's End. Only, as he began to paint the middle of the scene, something important was missing: Morgan's mother. She pointed the omission out to Eli.

"I know she's not there," Eli said. "I can't see her."

"What?" Morgan grabbed his arm to stop him from finishing the painting. "I can describe her for you, brother. What I've seen of her in my dreams, anyway. That has to be good enough."

"That's not how it works," Eli said. "You know that. I just draw what I see when I know where we want to go."

"You drew the younger Ochek when you wanted to see Ochek again!" Morgan said. "How's this any different?"

"I drew the picture that I saw in my head. He was in the picture." Eli put his hand on Morgan's hand and gently removed it from his arm. Continuing with the painting, he went on, "I know you want to see your mother. I'm thinking about this being the past. I'm thinking about you wanting to see your mother. This is what I'm seeing." He looked at her after making a brush stroke. "I believe she'll be there. Somewhere."

"Somewhere like where?! If this even works and it's the past and she's not there, if she's back at her house, there won't be a boat, you know. What am I supposed to do, swim to her house? In the river?"

"Maybe there'll be a boat." Eli kept going. The painting was almost finished. "Things usually work out."

"And if it doesn't just magically work out? If she's not there?"

"Then we'll be right here waiting for you," Emily said.

"Oh good," Morgan said, "for when I have another breakdown. If she's not there . . ."

"She'll be there," Eli assured Morgan.

"Oh, now you know, you don't just believe?" Morgan said.

"You said that you knew she'd be there, too," Eli said.

"That was before you drew a picture without her in it!"

"Morgan . . ."

Instead of carrying on the argument, Eli made one last stroke and the painting was finished. As soon as he'd completed it, the scene began to collapse into a tiny vortex, as it had before. Red retreated behind Eli again. The vortex grew until it was as big as the flat surface, and then the trapline appeared. The three of them, and a very cautious dog, inspected the trapline, the humans looking intently, the dog sniffing at the portal's entrance. Morgan thought it looked exactly the same as before. Had Eli opened a portal back to the present? Were they just going home? Her mother was nowhere in sight.

"So . . . I guess I'll just go look for her," Morgan said.

"We'll come with you and wait by the boulder," Eli said. "Otherwise the portal will close behind you and I'll have to draw everything all over again."

"What if I'm gone a long time?" Morgan asked. "It'll probably be earth time there, even if it's the past. Things won't go fast like on Askí."

"Then we'll wait a long time," Emily said.

"And if it's too late, and we don't have time to get back to Misewa?" Morgan asked.

"We know the portal's here," Eli said. "I'll start drawing World's End for when you come back so we'll have a bit more time to walk around."

Morgan took a deep breath, and then, with Emily and Eli and Red, she passed through the portal to the other side. As soon as they were through, the portal closed. They were relieved to see that there were still pointed white rocks on the ground that Eli could draw with.

"Does it feel like the past to you?" Morgan asked hopefully.

"Totally," Emily said.

"Go find your mom," Eli said.

"Okay." Morgan wiped some sweat from her palms onto her jeans. "Here I go."

She hugged Emily and Eli goodbye, then left them at the boulder. It was dusk, and the lingering light made it easier for Morgan to find her way to the clearing. She walked around the small lake, found the suggestion of a path, and followed it, with her ears and eyes peeled, because she didn't know where her mother would be. Maybe she was somewhere in the bush, hunting or picking berries. Maybe Morgan would bump into her on the path, her mother on her way to swim in the pond. Or maybe she'd be back in Norway House, and there'd be a canoe there for Morgan to use.

None of those possibilities turned out to be true.

When Morgan emerged from the path, she walked into the clearing and saw a woman sitting by the shore, looking out over the water.

THIRTY

By the looks of it, Jenny Trout hadn't brought much of anything with her to the land. A canoe pulled onto the rocks, right where the children had left their borrowed boat. The clothes on her back—jeans, a red flannel jacket with a gray hood, and a pair of moccasins with a bear claw design. A travel mug that somehow managed to stay upright, balancing on the rocks. It was chilly—it must have been autumn, hence the flannel jacket—and Morgan could see steam rising from the mug.

Morgan approached her mother quietly and slowly, not wanting to frighten or disturb her. She looked completely serene there on the shore, looking off into the distance. She stopped where the clearing ended and the shore began. She stared at her mother, while her mother stared at something else entirely. She didn't move or say anything for seconds that stretched into minutes, and then she cleared her throat loudly enough to get her mother's attention.

When Jenny turned around and her eyes met Morgan's, Morgan felt breathless. Her mother looked exactly as she had dreamed her, and Morgan knew, in that moment, that she'd been right all along: her dream had been a memory. The only difference was that her mother looked a bit older than she'd looked in Morgan's dream. There were a few lines on her face that had not been there before. There was sadness on her face that had not been there before.

"What are you doing out here?" her mother asked.

She looked around for another boat, but there was none.

"Just looking for something," Morgan said.

"All the way out here? Do you need help?"

"No, I found it."

"It's getting late," her mother said. "A girl that's young like you shouldn't be out here on her own."

"I can handle myself out here," Morgan said. "It's okay."

Her mother looked around again, as though she'd missed something before. "Where'd you come from?"

Morgan looked around, too. At the trees, the clearing, the water, the canoe, then her mother. "A long way away."

Her mother patted the rocks at her side. "Do you want to sit?"

Morgan took a deep breath in, then out. "I'd like that."

As soon as Morgan had sat down, had settled herself on the shore, had found a comfortable way to sit on the rocks, her mother picked up the travel mug and handed it to her.

"It's getting cold out. Have some."

"Thanks." Morgan took a sip. It was coffee. Black. "It's good." She handed it back to her mother.

"It's just instant coffee, my girl." She chuckled, then balanced the mug on the rocks again with steady hands, as though the calm they were sitting in had seeped into her being.

"I guess I like instant coffee," Morgan said.

"I guess you do."

They sat together in the quiet, and it was a comfortable quiet. Morgan was just happy to be there with her mother, a place she'd never thought she'd be. She didn't feel the need to say anything. It was enough just to sit with her, for her arm to touch her mother's arm, to taste the coffee she'd made, to just . . . be. They sat there, looking out over the water, until the sun had set. Morgan still didn't know what her mother was looking at, but after a while she thought that her mother might not be looking at anything at all, that she might have been lost in thought, as Morgan herself so often was. She liked that. She liked that they both drank coffee black. She liked that they both got lost in thought.

"What about you?" Morgan asked. "What are you doing out here?"

Her mother sighed. "I guess I'm looking for something too." She shook her head. "Or somebody."

"Somebody like who?" Morgan asked, and thought, *It's me, you're looking for me!* But that couldn't have been right.

How would her mother be looking for her out here, on the land? Whatever year it was, whenever Morgan had traveled to, the younger Morgan that lived in this time would never have been on the land. She would have been in the city somewhere, in one of the foster homes she'd stayed in. If her mother was looking for her now, she would have been in the city, not on a trapline. Morgan tried to hide her disappointment, but didn't have to. Her mother wasn't even looking at her. She'd not looked away from whatever her eyes were focused on.

Searching for something, somebody, just not Morgan.

"Seven years ago," her mother said, "I lost my girl. I didn't . . ." Her mother glanced at Morgan, then back at the same spot. "I didn't lose her, she was taken." She took a sip of coffee, and handed it to Morgan, who held it tightly but didn't drink any.

"I don't know why I'm even telling you this," her mother said.

"You can tell me," Morgan said.

Her mother sighed. She breathed in deeply, closed her eyes, then exhaled.

"She's in the system, somewhere. In Winnipeg, but that's all I really know. Some foster home, I guess. I know . . ."

Her mother's bottom lip quivered, then she held in the tears, something Morgan was not so good at. In fact, Morgan was crying right then, and she wiped the tears away, because to her mother she was a stranger, and so why would she be crying?

"I'll never stop trying to get her back. I . . . I just hope that she's okay, wherever she is."

Morgan knew that right then, somewhere in the city, the younger Morgan was not okay. But she didn't say that. She wanted her mother to have hope. So, she just listened.

"The thing is, when they took my daughter . . . it's always felt like they took me away, too. The person I used to be."

Her mother reached for the coffee mug, and their skin touched, just for a moment. In that moment, the dream Morgan had over and over again rushed into her mind. She remembered the feeling of being rocked by her mother, of looking up at her mother, of playing with her mother's long raven hair with her chubby fingers. Her mother took the coffee mug and sipped from it. Morgan watched steam rise from her mother's mouth, as though a soul that had been trapped for too long was finally being released.

"So, I come out here from time to time. I sit here, and I try to remember. Remembering is very important. It helps us to remember the stories we were gifted by our grandparents. Legends. Ways of living. Traditions. It helps us to remember who we are." She placed the travel mug onto the rocks. "I guess I'm out here trying to find . . . me. The me that I used to be, so that if . . . whenever . . . I see my girl again, I'll be the person she needs me to be. And maybe I can help her remember the person she is."

They sat beside each other. They stared out over the water. They both, Morgan thought, were trying to remember. Her mother sipped at the instant coffee she'd made, and for every sip she took, she offered one to Morgan. The rocks were uncomfortable, but the silence never was. The air was cold, but Morgan felt warm. The night grew darker, and the steam stopped rising from the travel mug. The stars were so much brighter than they ever were in the city. The stars looked as they did on Askí. Morgan looked up and found the Big Dipper, and pretended that it was Ochekatchakosuk. Gone, but not really.

Then her mother stood, brushed earth and fine white dust from the rocks off her pants.

"I'd better get back," her mother said. "My mother gets worried if I'm out too late, no matter how old I get."

"Yeah," Morgan said. "I'd better get back, too."

She started to get up, but in the process, her mother must have noticed the soles of Morgan's moccasins. The hole in one of them. How worn they were.

"You can't keep walking around out here with those things," her mother said, and without waiting for Morgan to respond, she began to take off her own moccasins with the bear claw design. She handed them to Morgan.

"I couldn't take those," she said.

"We'll trade," her mother said, "if that makes you feel better. Yours are pretty, and my mom can fix up the soles."

Morgan hesitated only a moment more, then accepted the footwear. She took off hers, gave them to her mother, and then both women put on their new moccasins.

"Ekosani," Morgan said.

Her mother smiled, took a few steps towards the canoe, then stopped. "My name's Jenny, by the way."

"I . . ." Morgan stumbled for the first time since seeing her mother. Now was the time. Now, she could tell her mother who she was. They could hug. They could talk about their lives. What her mother had done, where Morgan had been. They could sit on the rocks at the shore on the land all night, and she knew that Eli and Emily would wait for her. But then, at some point, they'd have to say goodbye. They'd say goodbye, and never see each other again. She'd done that once with Ochek, and she knew how much it hurt. She didn't think she could do that with her mother, and she didn't want to make her mother do that with her.

"I'm . . . really glad we met," Morgan said.

"I'm glad we met, too."

Her mother turned back towards the water, and Morgan watched until she had climbed into the canoe. She didn't think she could watch her mother paddle away, so she turned away as well, and walked towards the forest, towards the path. In the distance, by a boulder, Eli and Emily were waiting for her. But at the tree line, Morgan did look back. By then, her mother had begun paddling away.

"Jenny!" Morgan called out.

Her mother slowed the canoe and called back to Morgan, "Yes?"

Morgan felt her mother's arm rocking her. Morgan felt the land standing firm underneath her feet. Morgan felt her heart beat like a drum. *Thump. Thump. Thump. Thump. Thump. Thump. Thump.* She breathed in the fresh air. She breathed out. Her mother was sitting in the canoe, the stars above reflecting all around her, framed by the constellations.

"Kiskisitotaso," Morgan said.

EPILOGUE

When Morgan returned to the boulder, Eli and Emily were there. Eli gave her a hug. Emily gave her a hug, too, and then added a kiss on the cheek. Red was too busy chewing on a stick to care about the reunion. Eli had completed most of the illustration that would lead them back to Askí, miles east of Misewa, in World's End. He and Emily had been hanging out, and the boulder was waiting for one last mark from a pointed white stone. A stroke that, once all the hugs had been given, was made.

Instantly, the vortex appeared, and grew bigger and bigger still, sucking up the drawing Eli had created to reveal a real world in its place. Eli, with Red at his side, Emily, and Morgan stood at the opening of the portal, ready to cross over to the other world. It was late, but not too late, and they would have lots of time on Askí before having to come back to earth. In the morning, with Katie, they would take the road that curled around the right side of the community, park by the field, and then walk to Morgan's kókom's house.

Morgan thought about the morning, and the feast her kókom would make. She could almost smell the food. The hot bannock that would melt in her mouth, the fresh meat that had been caught straight off the land. She thought about all the places she'd been on Askí, in the North Country, and how all those adventures had brought her to where she was now. She thought about the places they had yet to go on the world they'd discovered. The past, the present, the future, all three dependent on each other, like strands in braided hair, like three kids about to take their first step on another adventure.

"It's a long way to Misewa," Eli said.

Morgan looked down at her mother's bear claw moccasins. She wiggled her toes inside them. They were small, but the leather would stretch. One day, they would be a perfect fit.

"When has a little walking ever stopped us?" she said.